WHIRL OF BIRDS

by

Liana Vrăjitoru Andreasen

Finishing Line Press
Georgetown, Kentucky

WHIRL OF BIRDS

Publisher: Leah Huete de Maines
Editor: Christen Kincaid
Cover Art: Leszek Kostuj, *Guardians of the Magic Garden VI*
Author Photo: Dmitry Zingerman
Cover Design: Elizabeth Maines McCleavy

Order online: www.finishinglinepress.com
also available on amazon.com

Author inquiries and mail orders:
Finishing Line Press
PO Box 1626
Georgetown, Kentucky 40324
USA

Contents

We have no bird in our hands, living or dead. We have only you and our important question. Is the nothing in our hands something you could not bear to contemplate, or even guess? Don't you remember being young when language was magic without meaning? When what you could say, could not mean? When the invisible was what imagination strove to see? When questions and demands for answers burned so brightly you trembled with fury at not knowing?

Toni Morrison, Nobel Lecture

My Big Man

Mm-bu. My big man. My big man protects me. My big man stands between us, little people, and the out there where wolves come from. When my big man out hunting, and my big woman out hunting, wolf grabs baby from our hiding place. I scream when wolf take baby. Big man follows tracks of wolf, with help from other big men. He kills wolf. Big woman helps them bring dead wolf back to small cave. Big man plays with us after hunting. He lets me pull at gray beard on his face, so I stop cry. Then all men and all women take flesh from wolf, to big cave. They make sparks with white rocks. Sparks make fire. When fire comes, big people and small people, all come. All eat. We scrape bones with sharp stone.

From cave mouth we see stars.

We little people stay together, from time of wake to time of wake to time of sleep. Only three of us little people now in small cave, after baby eaten. Big man brings baby wolf. He gives baby wolf to us, to play. Baby wolf plays a lot, chews bones. Then we eat baby wolf. We scrape bones with sharp stone again.

Some rain comes to rain in front of small cave. Many grays swell the sky. I still remember baby. I play when small cave is with light. I eat when big cave is with fire. I sleep when small cave full of dark. Now small cave full of cold, so sleep is harder.

My big man brings empty wolf to small cave. We sleep on empty wolf, is warmer now. I know: when cave full of cold, there will be white out there, soon. I remember the white from last time. And the time before last time. When white is out there, I remember, more hungry in small cave.

My big man comes back with wound on his arm. He moans, licks his arm. My big man stays in small cave many lights and darks. My big woman hunts more. Other big men bring some bones to us, paw from animal. Mushroom and nuts. My big man stays in small cave, makes more sharp stones. Ties sharp stone to thick stick. This stick not for fire, but for killing. I know killing. I see killing sometimes.

I climb on my big man's big back. I pull my big man's beard. His wound doesn't cry blood anymore.

Small whites come many times from sky. All white out there. I run out there. White is cold to touch. I run back in. I watch from small cave. When my big man gone hunting, he stays longer. My big woman goes hunting sometimes too.

When hungry, I go out of cave. Crow trapped, cannot fly. I catch crow myself—not my big man, not my big woman. I eat crow, give bones to little people in small cave.

My little people go play in big cave. I hide in small cave.

I know blood. Blood comes from dead. I make blood from under my belly, instead of yellow. Tastes like blood. My big woman drags me out there, from small cave. She walks around me many times. She washes with cold white under my belly. She drags me back to small cave. She pushes me from her. I cry, *"Mm-bu!"* Then again, *"Mm-bu!"* But my big man is not here.

My big man stays gone two lights and two darks. When he is back, dead deer hangs around his neck. His big body is full of coverings and warm. I cry and moan. I touch under my belly, and I show him my hand full of blood. He wraps warm arms around me and rocks me. My big man always gentle. Grunts gentle to us little people and says *"Ti-ko, Ti-ko."* I say, *"Mm-bu, Mm-bu,"* and I sleep in his arms. When I wake up, I'm in his arms and the fire is in front of me. Little people, big people eating. Fire makes red on their faces. Warm is good. I sleep again.

I have learned to mate. When I feel itch under my belly, I go to big cave. I look for little men. The little-little ones don't want to play mate. When I find a little man that does, we hide behind rocks in cave. Mate makes me warm.

Ice sticks in front of cave begin to drip. Puddles now. The yellow in the sky is warmer. Big cave fire is smaller now. Only for food. My big man plays with my little people in small cave. Doesn't play with me. I watch them play. We all sleep alone again, in small cave.

When cave is full of light, I want to mate. There is one man now. A man who growls, scratches and beats the others. Mates with me. Bigger man, no hair on his face. I run to him now. I say, *"Nya!"* He says, *"Nya!"* We mate in dark too. My man.

My big man watches my man. My man growls at my big man. I run out there with my man, out of cave. Mate in the small new grass. Mate by river. We kill and eat things.

I don't go back to cave for many lights and darks. I go everywhere with my man now. We sleep hidden in bushes. We wake if there's growl. We growl back. My man sharpens stones, to make killing stick. He gave me new killing stick. We track deer. We run, we run. We kill together. We eat raw.

We sleep in small cavern. Safe to sleep here. We pull bushes at the cavern mouth. I want to be with my man, in the out there. I want to mate forever, with my man.

The out there is big now. Sky is bigger than from cave mouth. Stars are many. More and more woods where we go. We follow river. Woods never end. We climb hill, sit on rocks, in the wind. We clean in river and we drink. Water plays, so we play with water. Water shows my face, two eyes with sky color in them. I open mouth and the face in water opens mouth.

Sometimes my man gets fish with killing stick. Bear gets fish, no killing stick. We stay away from bear, because only two of us.

My belly is big now. There's something inside, under my skin. I feel something I know is alive. I know I want it to come out. My big woman had belly like this, before baby. I don't want to mate. My man says "*Nya!*" and I huddle behind big tree. My man finds me. My man mates me. I try to run away, and he growls. I want my big man protect me.

I follow river back, and my man follows me. I want back in big cave, small cave. I want my big man. I want my big woman. I want to play with my little people. My belly moves.

Some lights and darks pass and I recognize trees and sky in front of rock hill where cave is. I run. My man runs, grabs my arm, makes me stop. I growl, and he points ahead, to big cave mouth. I crouch on ground, fast. Danger. Big danger. Wind brings smell of blood. I back up, hide behind big bush. Thorns make my arms hurt. My belly moves.

We move with little steps, hiding all the time, crouching. Danger and blood smells are ahead. Movement in front of cave mouth. Big women, big men. Then I see the bigger men. I never see them before. Their heads are higher than the big men I know. Shoulders thin. Hairs short. More skins wrapped around their bodies. Long spears in their hands. Throw long spears to people in my cave. Little people killed, enemy men grab little dead people. Enemy grab dead big people in my cave. Enemy many, many.

Enemy people too. But enemy faster, with cunning. My people die.

I see my big woman. Dragged outside cave by enemy. I growl, lift my head above bush, and my man pulls me down. "*Mm-a! Mm-a!*" I say. I have trembling in all my body. My face is wet. My eyes swim with water. I can tell death even from a distance. My big woman dead.

They will eat our dead. We eat our dead too, sometimes. If hunger is long.

My man pulls me away. I don't see my big man dead, at the cave. Where is my big man? Is he away? Stay away.

I will stay away. We sleep in deep bushes. I hear many things, and trembling comes back sometimes. After this one dark, we return to watch, and see enemy at the cave. They bring their women. Their little people. The cave is theirs now.

We follow river again, look for small cavern under the rocks. We stay there two lights, two darks without coming out. We hear enemy sometimes. They are many. They hunt. We hear their shouts, animal death screams. We do not dare come out of cavern even when light is out there.

My belly hurts. My legs wet. The living thing wants to come out. I scream, and my man pushes hand on my mouth. Enemy close. We can smell them. I try to make no sound, but sound comes out. Baby comes out. Skins fall around baby, and we eat skins. Hunger is strong.

Hunger is very long now. My man goes out to look for food, comes back quickly. He points out there, shows me height of enemy and I know he means enemy close. We die if enemy finds us. I feed baby so baby won't make sounds. Baby clings to my breast.

Baby has hunger, because my breasts are dry. My man is gone again, but I fear enemy will see him. Maybe he can find rabbit. Crow. Baby deer. I eat moss. I eat worms from under the rocks.

I go out there, to look for more worms. I listen. I hear baby make sounds in the cavern, but I must eat first. I find a root and I eat. Baby sounds stop.

I run to cavern. Stay away, enemy.

My man is with baby. Baby limp. Head dangling, from where my man holds baby. I try to reach baby, to take baby from his hands, but my man growls. My man bites limp baby and growls more. I want my big man to kill this man, but my big man is nowhere. Where can I find my big man? Can I make baby alive again? I know death is forever. I run.

I run, and I run. I will run more. I only stop to drink from river. I will run forever. Enemy behind me—enemy that I see, enemy that I don't see. My man is enemy now.

Not my man anymore.

I have to keep running, find a cave. Leave that cave, find another. I will look for people, short and strong, not long and enemy. I want to look for my big man, to protect me. Sorry I left my big man and cave, and my mate man is traitor. Eats baby. My big man still alive? My big man in woods somewhere? Never go back to big cave. If he alive, he never at the cave either.

Enemy everywhere now, and I have to be careful forever. Eat when I can. Many roots and worms, sometimes an animal.

I don't know if I find my big man again. I know death will come, when enemy finds me.

I know big enemy will win the out there, forever. This place will be enemy forever.

I don't know it at this moment, and I will never know it, but there's something in me that has settled into the course of things. I await the lurking death out there, though I don't know how it will come. Although I don't know it except with the fear and relief that live in me forever, leaves will cover me wherever I fall, wherever the rest of me falls that doesn't perish fast. Years will cover me and the big yellow up above will shine just the same. Many steps will fall over the earth that sits on top of me. Things that I know and I have words for will soon have other words. Other words will grow big as the out there, big as the sky. Everything will be enemy named, soon. The cold white will fall from the sky and melt, fall from the sky and melt, and children of children of children of enemy will have words for the melting too.

My big man will be lost to me. But I will keep looking.

And this, I don't know yet: the traces of me will soon know that we are not really lost. Our traces will be out there. And maybe you, one day, you, the child of the child of the child of enemy, you will find my big man. A bone of him, a bone of me, a sharpened stone and the ash of our fire. You will smell our death without smelling our blood, and you will shiver in your bones, where you will know that something lives, yet unnamed. You, too, will feel settled into the course of things.

I have no words to leave behind, but you will see my traces.

Perhaps you will think of a story to put me back together. My dead baby. My big man. Perhaps you will say that the enemy was better than me, and you will have many words to say it with, and the traces to show why. Perhaps you will know why the enemy chased us off into a long hunger from which there's no return. My big man will fit into your naming of Neander-Thal.

But when you become wiser than the undoubted proof of these traces, then perhaps you will know how I was here. Perhaps you will look into the mirror of the river and see my mouth opening and closing—a distant image to bring us closer. Eons from now, you will know that my big man was a gentle man.

The Puppet Show

In his workshop, a lamp gave faint, drunken light. His fingers, swollen by alcohol, searched through the velvet and muslin strewn among buckets. Pieces of wood lay shapeless on the floor, and he picked the precise ones he needed. He set to work. First, a face took shape from layers of papier-mâché. The skin was rough. The nose grew squarely out of the face. Lips turned red under the brush. They were not meant to move. The wide painted eyes stared into the dark.

The body, light. One arm dangled aimlessly, waiting for a string. Hard plastic on the wrists. The fingers stuck tightly together, ready to wave and dangle with modulated pathos. The legs hopped without a body until screws set them in place. Head and body united for the first time, and the shadow of wood and cloth became somewhat human.

The theater itself was old. Italian-style columns, baroque statues, double stairs of marble and gilded cherubs on the ceiling—it had all of that. His workshop was at the back of the building, away from the glamor, though he did not mind at all. Art in its powdered, vestigial parody, filled with ancient desires, was just another form of denial. He was not there to glorify the empty laughter of swelled corsets and glittering wigs. In the miniature amphitheater hidden past the actors' dressing rooms, past cold corridors, he put together a story for children. It was a story like no other: it had no end. Child after child returned every week for the free show, and he was certain they were there to know. They did not mind that he was a drunkard, because the truth he concocted week by week thrilled them, changed them, filled them with lights and shadows before they returned to their parents.

In the story, Gina was always the main character—a frail, blonde princess whom the children adored. The actress had grown up in the city and she wanted to leave it, but having a job was better than having a dream. The puppeteer wanted her to keep her own name in the story, so she accepted. The only other human actor in the show was to be played by one of the puppeteer's friends. He would always be called Radu, no matter which of his friends he brought there for the role.

The rules to the story were simple: Gina would not ask questions. She would read and rehearse her part for that week, but she was never allowed to know what the puppets were going to do, or what Radu was there for. She'd tell her story to the children, then she would wait. Small animals would come to her. Storms would come and go. She was allowed to move around—and to smile. The curtain would fall and stay closed for ten seconds, and she would catch her breath. Then, she would tell the second story and let the puppets and the strings do the rest. At the end of each performance she was instructed to speak one single word—she could choose any word. It just had to make sense to the children.

Gina the princess is lost in the woods. She calls for her sisters and they do not answer. Her face is pale. The light from two reflectors rests on her with longing, on her white dress and her long hair falling on her shoulders like yellow satin. Silk flies across the stage—the wind. She asks the wind to listen to her story, to take pity and find her sisters. The story is sad, for her sisters have gone to the witches' lair. They had been turned to stone. Gina sings and the wind of silk wraps around her body. Trees move across the stage and she falls asleep in the arms of the wind. The curtain falls.

Gina the princess wakes up and there are three kings hanging on strings. They come from the past. The one who founded the country is old as the centuries. The one who defended the country has a golden coat and a sword. The one who unified the country is solemn and bearded. The princess tells the kings how she lost her sisters, and she sings again. But now her song is different, of sacrifice: for the good of the country, she will not look for her sisters anymore.

Now Radu has come on stage. His eyes are like fire, and he dances with her. The children applaud. She is smiling.

Yet the play is not over. Radu lets go of her hand and runs through the trees. Gina cannot call him back, for she is not allowed to speak. Her face distorts as if she knows something terrible, something that even Radu does not know yet. A cardboard train comes clumsily onstage, with human feet trotting instead of wheels. He jumps in front of it and falls, and the train carries him behind the curtain.

She looks at the children. Holding their breaths, they are waiting for the word.

LOSS, she says. Some children start crying.

Marcus played the role of Radu this time. He had been playing it for over a month now, though it didn't pay much.

Marcus had been a long-time friend of the puppeteer's, and the two liked to talk over vodka. With low, dreamy voices they would speak of Schopenhauer, misery, the will to live, and the lie of love. The communists were not averse to drunks, and vodka was a cheap import anyway. Marcus knew German words and the puppeteer laughed and gestured wildly toward an empty sky. Marcus talked of the deception that love is, the emptiness of desire, which he could name in German: *Wunsch*. Vodka was the drink of the working class, and the two felt raw and free in the dark and smoky taverns, where workers drank and cursed the history to which their misery bound them. After a few drinks, the puppeteer and his philosopher friend tingled with compassion for the workers caught in reality's dream, and sang along when drunken songs burst throughout the tavern. In the morning, the workers would return to their factories.

It was the puppeteer who encouraged Marcus to ask Gina out.

"With her, love is not a lie," the puppeteer would say. He would grin, his face glistening with sweat.

Mostly, Marcus took her to cafes, buying her cheap cake and coffee.

Just a few days after the last show, Marcus threw himself in front of the train. In a letter to Gina, he was angry and jealous, and she cried until her eyes had no more tears. She did not learn her lines that week and the show was cancelled.

The puppeteer brought her flowers. In her apartment building, everyone knew him. They were surprised he was not staggering this time, and she was surprised he did not ask her for money.

"Drink tea with honey for your voice," he pleaded.

She wondered who would play Radu now, but he told her she would meet him soon.

The new Radu was named Matei. Also a friend of the puppeteer, Radu had opened his door one day to hear him ask, "Wouldn't you like to try your hand at acting? Just once a week, and you won't have many lines. You'll meet Gina."

Matei had come from the country. Like many sons of peasants after the great collectivization, he had no ambitions to get noticed on the combine harvester and receive medals for milking cows. He'd come to the city to study. He wrote, he published, he had expansive plans. He knew French perfectly, and he could recite poems of Paul Verlaine, the absinthe-dream-poet whose friend, Rimbaud, led him to his ruin. He told stories of Verlaine's wife, a woman with small hands and vast anger.

Matei loved the puppeteer and dragged him along when he and his fellow students gathered to read their stories of robots and other planets. The robots in their stories had grand ideas of uniting all countries and making everyone equal. The other planets looked strangely familiar, except they worked perfectly, until they didn't work perfectly anymore. Most of the stories ended in great explosions and revolts, fought by people who did not want to be equal.

In a country drowned in secrecy and fear, people loved stories of robots and other planets. Matei tried to convince the puppeteer to make robot marionettes and transform his little stage into another planet.

"Think how much the children would love that," Matei insisted.

The puppeteer shook his head and told him the actress wanted to be a princess, and the children wouldn't understand science fiction.

Matei asked about the death of Marcus, because the puppeteer had introduced them vaguely one time. Some people said Marcus' death had been an accident. Some said he had been pushed.

"It's very sad," the puppeteer shook his head.

When Matei became Radu, Gina let him make her smile, and she even started laughing when he carried her in his arms around the stage. Nobody noticed that the puppeteer had stopped drinking. He went to lunch with the two of them, and he watched avidly, looking deep into their eyes where he could see that, unbeknownst to the actors of the puppet show, their souls were already dancing together. And Gina was finally able to stop crying.

Spring came, and Gina was in love. She quieted some nameless fear in her and, on stage, she made the children laugh, waiting for Radu.

Gina the white princess eats peaches. She makes believe the giant peaches are real, even if their color is bright, plastic orange. Hungry, the children imagine the taste as they roll their tongues in their mouths. Gina is not sad anymore. Her song is spring, like outside. Her white dress sparkles with the promise of a happy story, even if she is enclosed in a giant bird cage. She eats peaches with hope. She sings of the land that was frozen by a North Pole sorcerer. Outside her cage, little rabbits and ducks are trapped in ice. She summons warm rains to fight the ice. When her song ends, clouds begin to dance in front of her. It rains, and the rabbits jump out from the ice. The ducks fly. They free her from her cage and the curtain falls.

In ten seconds, the curtain lifts again.

The children listen to her song, waiting for Radu. For the last few weeks, he has been carrying her in his arms and has been giving her fist-sized rubies and diamonds. Now the children are whispering his name. Surrounded by flying marionettes, slashing the heads off rubber dragons, he moves valiantly towards the princess and her rabbits. She is sitting by a big tree. He sees her, and his face is round and laughing. His eyes are blue in the spotlight. She waves to him, but she cannot talk anymore. He stops. She stands up and lifts her arms.

There is a flash of lightning. He looks up: the tree bursts in flames and falls upon him. The princess screams and rushes forward, but the flames have vanished. So has Radu.

The children gasp. She has to give them a word now, but she is crying again. They are so close that they can see her tears fall on the dusty wooden floor.

DEFEAT, she says, and runs off the stage.

She became very afraid that day. She tried to talk to the puppeteer after the show, but he was drunk again, and he was asking for money. She pleaded with him.

"Is something going to happen? You have to stop it," she said.

He stumbled in front of her, and it seemed as if his thoughts also stumbled in the dust of his mind.

"You love him, you love him," he chanted in his drunkenness. "L'amour toujours!" he sang.

Matei left that week to visit his parents in the country. The weather was capricious, and there were powerful storms in May. Lightning hit a big tree just as he was trying to load wood into a cart, somewhere remote outside the village. He died instantly.

Gina refused to go to work for a month. The puppeteer crawled on his knees at her door, but she would not let him in.

Then came Laurian. Unlike the one before, he did not care to ask questions. He knew of the deaths. He knew Gina from school. When the puppeteer asked him if he would play Radu, he said yes, and that he'd talk to Gina himself.

In her little apartment, Gina was dressed in black. She stared at the man at her door and sudden memories came flooding. She blinked, averted her eyes, and waved for him to come inside. He came strolling in, tall and thin and the devil may care. She just stood there, unable to ask him if he wanted a drink, or what he wanted.

He sat down. His body rigid, a faint smile fluttered across his face. He watched her tremble. Minutes passed before he spoke:

"I'm not afraid, and you need the money. Come play the princess again."

"Do you remember..." she began, but then was silent.

"There isn't much to remember," he said. "We never spoke in school."

"We danced. Once."

"We did. I am going to play Radu, with or without you."

"But the others..."

He stood up and turned to leave. He opened the door.

"Wait!" Her voice resounded in the stairwell. "I will be there," she murmured, as in a trance. "You can tell him I'm coming back. But I will never speak to him again."

It took her a long time before she could make herself go back inside. Standing in the door, her long yellow hair hung like silk.

Gina the white princess has finished her story. Today, it is about a small boy hiding in a cave as the world is crumbling. The princess is picking a flower. It is a big flower—velvet and rubber on a thick wire stem. She lets the first row children touch it. Small fingers caress the large petals. It is dark in the room, and the children are cold. There is no heat so they keep on their worn-out coats.

Gina the white princess waltzes in front of the cardboard castle. She seems to be waiting for someone, and a bird flies past her above the children's heads. The children chirp. They applaud and their hands are cold. There is thunder and the boy-marionette shivers in the cave. Then the boy finds a book under a rock, and the boy falls asleep with his head on the white pages. The curtain falls. It opens again after ten seconds.

Gina the white princess sings to the children about the spell someone put on her long ago, and now she appears in the dream of a lonely puppet-boy. Strings come down from the ceiling with a witch that dances with jolts, and her orange foam face shines. The children understand evil. Their parents curse and spit, so a boy lets out a crooked word for the crooked witch. Something in the white princess recoils, but she cannot let them know she heard it, for she is ethereal and beautiful. There are footsteps backstage and the maroon curtain moves. The children can see someone is coming but they pretend to be surprised. The new Radu comes out. He looks like the sleeping boy, except he is tall, his long face defiant. The strong, happy Radu is gone, and for a month there hasn't been a show at all. This Radu moves slowly, as if the small stage will take forever to cross. He looks the princess in the eye and the children see her blush in the spotlight. He takes the book from her hand and says thank you. He turns around, and the book bursts into flames. He leaves the stage without a glance back.

Alone, Gina the princess is crying.

NEVER, she tells the children.

She swore she would never love again. Laurian did not bring her flowers, did not ask her to go for coffee, did not say more than hello and goodbye. The puppeteer invited them both to his house, but she would not speak to either of them, and she would not go. The puppeteer drank more than ever. When she came to rehearse, he would tell her stories of his travels with the Roma people. Stories of a secret society. Stories of his two children, one in Russia and one in Poland. She would look at him with wide blue eyes, and she would not answer at all. Sometimes Laurian would come to the rehearsals, just to watch her from the shadows. The puppeteer would take him by the shoulders, push him to where she was sitting and reading. The two refused to look each other in the eye, and the puppeteer would laugh with alcohol breath.

"You are meant to be together! You are made for love!"

It meant nothing.

Outside, in the streets, people mumbled louder, sometimes within earshot of the police. Dirty streets, empty stores. Dubbed movies from the West played to smoking crowds in dingy basements.

That was where she saw Laurian by chance, watching a horror movie with rubber monsters killing beautiful actors. It was as if they had no choice but to walk home together, through streets of fall with flying papers and bags. That was when he squeezed her chin with his fingers until it hurt, and he kissed her carelessly, recklessly. Her eyes asked for a sign, but in the cold air his eyes did not speak.

She feared the show the following night. She did not want to go. She put on her boots of fake leather, and her coat of fake fur, and she let her feet take her through the streets.

Her voice is shaking as she tells her first story. The children do not notice. They are hungry when they look at the long table filled with plastic food.

Her fingers shake as she pretends to eat a fat turkey leg that looks more like the leg of an ostrich.

Her hands and her legs are in chains. She stares blankly as the curtain falls, and she counts to ten.

She is still in chains as she begins the second song, the second story. The children cannot hear her and they ask each other what she said. Radu! Radu! they shout, for who else can free her, and who else will share in the plastic feast?

Behind the curtain, the puppeteer watches, and Laurian watches him watch.

"Go onstage!" whispers the puppeteer. "Now!"

"I quit."

"You what?"

"I'm leaving."

Laurian turns in the dark and walks away. The puppeteer is furious, and the children can hear his drunken curses. The puppeteer throws a cloak on and rushes onstage. No one can see his face. He pulls the chains away from the princess, cursing her. Gina the princess is frozen. She cannot move. He slaps her.

"The word, give them the word!" he whispers through the cloak.

"The word!" the children shout.

She stands up.

DEATH, she says loud and clear. She pushes him and runs off the stage.

Blood flowed in the street that week. The whole country boiled with the anger of many years. That week, a dictator was stunned that people stopped following orders. Even the secret police did not help him. Like puppets with their strings hanging loose, they were just waiting to see where the dice would fall. The dictator was run off his palace, and the palace crumbled.

The puppeteer's liver was swollen from drinking, and he stopped going to work. He died a few months later. His mother asked relatives to help bury him. She had no money. She had always given him all she'd had.

Laurian did not die. Like many, he started his own business; like many, he became rich. He sponsored the theater and helped renovate the ancient Italian-style building. Great shows were to follow. Few people could afford them.

The marionettes were all locked up in wooden chests and thrown into the theater's attic. Like memories, they lived on.

The small amphitheater where puppet shows used to be staged was turned into offices. There, a new political party gathered weekly, and it brought many young people with many ideas. They drank truth and justice with water. In a year, there were fewer people coming to the meetings, and finally the offices were sold to another political party. This one lasted two years, changing leadership. People felt used. People felt betrayed. The party split into factions.

In the end, the place was fully remodeled to house a private school for actors.

As for Gina, she left the country and became an actress somewhere without puppets.

The story of Gina the princess was never finished. The children did not dare cry or ask if there would ever be another show. Gina the princess lingered like a scar in their memories. They whispered her name to each other for years.

Like their parents, the children did not know what they should or shouldn't remember. The memories would sort themselves out on their own.

Stolen Light

When his father had come from Santa Fe and took him to see the volcanoes around Albuquerque, they didn't talk much.

The man's two wide-eyed girls blushed and said something like hi to him, and he said something like hi to them. They walked behind their father on the dirt path, looking skittishly at the boy and elbowing each other. They seemed relieved when the half-brother stayed behind, to climb the rocks blackened by millions of years. The grim man walked ahead, while the two small bouncing figures stopped for petroglyphs, circling the boulders like lizards. The boy stretched flat on the rough, dark surface of long extinguished lava, sniffing the burning air. His eyes floated over the distance as he watched the trinity of strangers, and he made voices for them in his head, talking of school and of kittens, never of him. In the end, the man's silhouette ushered the girls back through the dried shrubs, to the parked car.

He took a small lava rock with him. After that day, he let his hair grow. He made believe he had Paiute blood, imagining a time when there were no city lights to drown the desert. Once, an ocean lived there.

When he cornered his mother, finally daring to ask the questions brewing in his mind for too long, she said his father's family did not owe him a thing, and that Santa Fe was the other whore city. Now thirteen, he thought he knew what she meant, but he didn't. His mother's eyes narrowed with a distant scorn and she said he should go live with his father if he missed him so much. Then she laughed as she watched him plait his hair at the back of his head—her laugh not mean, just puzzled. She teased that girls at school would let him gossip with them. Jose Angel, she said, you don't really want to be their girlfriend, do you? Your face is not square enough to carry braids like a man.

He became more quiet and graceful when he learned to play guitar. The notes, discordant at first, began to paint new colors on the mountain that stretched in front of his window. While everyone else came back with stories from tourist-cluttered Spring Mountain at the West of town, he had bound himself to the heart of Sheep Range Mountain, where secrets and hidden forests lay. He hummed to it at sunset, and it responded—ancient and bloodied by the sun—sending echoes through the ageless air, and sharp voices of desert buzzards. At night, the lights from the Strip would suddenly spread their blue-yellow shadows over the city's edge, and his guitar would be silent again.

When the dark cloud came over Las Vegas, it cooled off the old, yellow skin of the mountain. The antelopes and wild goats must be grateful, he thought, looking at the peaks in the distance. He could almost feel the relief in the wide nostrils, no longer forced to breathe in the flames of the summer air. It wasn't even the time for rain, for the heavy heat of the Nevada August melted the asphalt, blending it with the smell of garbage, dust, and old drywall. The cloud did not bring water.

As much as he welcomed the cloud during the day, he started to hate it in the evening, and more so when he saw the cloud was there to stay. At dusk, the heavy, crawling monster in the sky obliterated the orange warmth of the setting sun, so the mountaintop grew gloomy. He waited a few days, a week, and then he waited more. His eyes were humid like the air was, it seemed, for the first time since the dawn of ages.

The cloud did not give back the mountain: it sat over the city like a breathing, lazy presence, while its edges churned and spat black vapors over the closest peak. His mother brought home people's worried guesses, and Jose Angel brought home the children's version of the apocalypse.

His mother was wrong about one thing: girls loved to play with his long hair, and the soft look he gave them from beyond thin glasses made them dream. They did not want him to be their girlfriend. His mother sighed, not knowing that the kids at his school were not the ones she had grown up with. Above all, she could not sense from him just how much faster the looming cloud was making their young blood boil. Something in them pushed forward, eager to cross all the paths they could cross, as if afraid that life was even shorter than their parents always said.

Leaning on the wall by the main entrance, Jose Angel watched the sway of hips across the schoolyard. There was less grace, more cleverness in that motion than in the flight of antelopes. He chose to ignore the distant judgment of the mountain. A fist landed on his shoulder and he turned, smiling vaguely.

"Hey man," Stoneface grunted, absently looking up at the cloud.

"Hey," he said, his eyes returning to the girl in tight pants and high heels.

"Jose's got a girlfriend," shouted Jimmy, quicker than Stoneface in following his glance to where the girls were giggling.

"We're still on tonight in my garage?" he asked, instantly resenting Jimmy's knowing grin. "Sal said we can use his guitar today."

"Your neighbor's cool. But no, I can't tonight," Jimmy said. "You don't know what's going on at all?"

"Like what?" he mumbled.

"The cloud!" The answer seemed obvious. "They're talking about government intervention. There's something *really* going on!"

Jose Angel shrugged.

Stoneface's fist hit his shoulder again.

"Jose, are you insane?" he hissed in his ear. "Everybody's talking. There's something in that cloud for sure! Something *will* happen!"

"Rain?" he said, and Jimmy's laughter sounded like a cough, in surprise. Jose's eyes returned to the girl in tight pants. Short, slim, perfect face. A hard face of a girl who could crush with no remorse. The best challenge.

"Rain? Rain?" Jimmy shouted. "Stop bullshitting. You must've heard what's happening. Your mom's a nurse, she must hear... scientists and such..."

"Yeah, people talk about aliens," he said, looking at his friend to see if that was really what he wanted to talk about.

"That too, but maybe worse than that! My mom says even *atheists* are convinced now. Come on, man, it's Las Vegas of all cities! Of course there's a connection."

"With the aliens?" he said scornfully.

"End of days! Something like that! You know, what they said was supposed to happen in 2021. Maybe the Aztec gods were just a little late, you know. Or maybe Jesus..."

"So what you want me to do? Go confess that I've been playing music?"

"It's not about confessing, man," Stoneface said with premature wisdom, winking at Jimmy.

"Why am I supposed to worry about judgment day?" he answered, starting to sound annoyed.

"You're telling me you really want to die a virgin? In Las Vegas?" said Stoneface, fluttering a grin. "Let me tell you something. How much money you got?"

"Leave him alone, he can do my sister for free!" laughed Jimmy. "Come on, you can even find whores on discount. They say the cloud's worsening the inflation, so they're desperate."

Jose Angel's eyes flew back to the girl, in spite of himself. She was watching him now, too far to hear.

"Exactly," said Jimmy, surveying the exchange with triumph. "See, that's what *you* should be doing. You don't need our help. But I for one have other plans if I'm going to be dying soon.

"Like what?"

"They said they might be closing the school. For a while at least..."

"And?"

"And...! What do you mean and! It's the end of the world, come on! We can burn"—he whispered— "burn the school down and nobody would even care!"

Even Stoneface was startled.

"See? Way ahead of you two," said Jimmy.

"Well, let's go, my mom's probably here. But this weekend we've got to do something... something really cool, "Stoneface muttered conclusively. "Let's meet up at Floyd –"

"That's lame, at the park? Let's go to the Air Force Base," said Jimmy.

"No, at the park, usual place. Maybe I'll bring something," Stoneface said turning away.

And they scattered—to parked cars and to parents with worries on their faces. The cloud loomed over the cars and parents, and over the streets onto which they had scattered.

Sunday morning he woke up with the certainty that something was going to happen. He had dreamed of the cloud, and it had been one of those dreams where everything is swallowed up by everything—the sky and the ground merge and there's an unmistakable, sinking feeling of the end of the world. Perhaps the news his mother kept watching with solemn confusion had gotten to him at last. Or maybe the new prophets at street corners, drooling with delight to see the darkness over the city, had seeped into his mind like so many city dreams.

In truth, he had told the girl to meet him today, instead of joining his friends. Could they be right, he wondered, that he really had to take all he could from the world, as if he had hours to live, minutes? And what if it was true, what they said, that this city was not worth it, that this world was not worth it? Yet what right did that thing inside the cloud have, to take the mountain and the sunlight too? Little by little, even the night lights were going away, as if the darkness of the primordial ocean were lying in wait, ready to reclaim the earth.

When he reached her, the girl was sitting on the bench. She watched him with bemused detachment, eyeing him with the certainty that he had to know she'd chosen his invitation over others, many others. Yet there was something shy in how she looked at him too.

The end of the world pushed him forward, making him smile and speak faster. They walked past Tartan Elementary, and he pointed it out to her, as if the few years that had passed since he was an angry child could explain the dreaminess of his impatient adolescence. She glanced at the school, glanced at him, half listening. She wore makeup.

"Look," she laughed over his unfinished sentence. "The bio teacher. In that car."

Something pierced the inside of his chest, as if a secret had come out. Not that he really liked that teacher, with her face of rain and deer, and her books about mountains. Not that she might see him and wonder why this girl, of all girls. Not that a remote smell of secret forests and lava and millions of years lifted with the dust in the wake of the car. He just froze, and he dropped the girl's hand, feeling sudden coolness on his palm.

"So which bus are we taking? To the Strip?" the girl said, looking into his uncertain eyes.

"I thought we'd walk for a while," he said, his eyes turning to the darkened top of the mountain, where the gray cloud was boiling as if ready to rain.

"You want to kiss me, don't you," said the girl, taking his hand again.

Her face was close now, and her warm lips searched his. He thought of his guitar, and then he could think of nothing.

It was then that the idea hit him—as if he could hear with absolute clarity the voice of the mountain, and everything was made bright in that illumination. It was still early in the day, and he was certain now that there was a spring somewhere on his mountain. Maybe in the Secret Forest. With the Western Mountains so close, so green, not many would hike up North, except someone's hippy brother or someone's crazy relative from out of town. He could go unbothered past the cloud, past the first peak, and he could find the light that had been lost. Everything started to feel like the end of the world, and everything felt like the beginning of the world.

Maybe he could find new music for his guitar that the cloud had silenced. Or maybe he could just keep walking, and he would have a new story to tell, every day to eternity.

When Jose Angel's mother called, worried to death, the girl said they had just walked for a few hours, and they had had lunch, nothing else. She said he'd left her by her house and he'd walked on. She did not know why he was not home that evening, or that night, or the next morning. His friends did not know. Even his father called. The girl could not give a new answer to the strange man who talked of "my son," when everyone knew Jose as the son of a single mother. The police asked questions, and more questions after a few days, but in the end they seemed more concerned about the cloud, and about keeping their jobs. Look, they would say, we don't have the budget to look for him. City's been losing tourists. People's pockets are empty, and who's going to care about Las Vegas.

The kids at school knew the cloud had taken their friend. They did not dare mention aliens to their parents, but they were certain. Stories swirled under the shadow of the cloud, and Jimmy did not burn down the school. The city lights were dimmer every night. Many people lost sleep. Jose Angel's mother had lost everything.

In early September, when the helicopters and the planes arrived to crisscross, unseen, the obstinate cloud, his mother thought her endless petitions had made somebody care enough to send help. He could still be alive after two weeks—he was a good kid, a gentle kid. Maybe he'd become amnesic, gone crazy from that cloud, run away. She stopped and talked to the prophets—more of them every day—and they saw her son on white clouds, on white horses, on something white, on light. There was nothing white in Las Vegas, but they were happy about that. Evil is up there, it drove your son away, they said. She listened to them and prayed harder. Jose Angel was still gone.

She accused the father. He accused the mother. The new wife. The cloud. The school. Social services sniffed around for abuses, psychologists looked for diaries with drawings. Everyone remembered the soft eyes that searched for more, that were never quite in tune with everyone. The guitar became the symbol of his torment. They thought his hair was a sign. They thought he bought into this new religion, joined a sect. Stole a car. Had a secret life making money at the few casinos that kept their doors open.

There were sightings of him, with a blonde, with a brunette. At his age! Heads shook, prayers washed his soul clean. The cloud was evil.

With the new year dawning, an old man came on foot from the highway. He strolled through the neighborhood with a childish air of searching, and everyone thought they'd hear a new prophecy. He seemed surprised to see the cloud still there, but he smiled to himself and pointed at the sky as if a prankster resided above. On Big Bear Drive, his steps were hesitant and, when he reached Jose Angel's house, he stood there a long time in front of the gate. Finally, the crying mother came outside, ready to curse his gods and the cloud they had brought.

He smiled, with the eyes of a child.

"I have a message," he said, and his voice was soft, timeless. He seemed startled to see her stare at him blankly.

"Everyone has a message," she hissed.

"I know about your son," he said, and his words trembled slightly.

"And what did God say?" she scorned, turning around.

"No," he said, and this time his voice was knowing. "It's not that at all."

She stopped. Something struck her, like a light behind her, an incomprehensible recognition.

"What?" she said, shaking. "What do you know?"

"Your son is alive. But he will not return."

"Where is he?" she roared, turning to face the man, with wild eyes.

"I am just a messenger," he said, watching her deeply, taking in her desperation. "He will always love you," he whispered, lost in memories.

Her eyes watered. The old man turned to leave. She grabbed his arm, and he pulled it. She beat him with his fists, she screamed, and he pulled himself away. He was not weak.

The woman ran inside and grabbed her phone, feverishly dialing numbers, missing, dialing again. She ran to her car, talking to the police at the same time, and she drove out, where she thought she had seen him going. She did not find him. The police did not find the stranger either. Sirens screamed and flashed amidst a city that had lost its lights, and the mother spent a frantic night in one police car after another.

That night, the old man returned to the house one more time. He could tell she was not there and his night shadow went unseen.

With trembling hands, he let himself into the house, surprised he did not even have to think. The dogs did not bark. He wanted one thing only—something that he could keep without guilt, something to let him remember. It belonged to him, and he would make it sing the nebulous stories of the lifetime he carried with him.

She would find the note where the guitar had been, and she would cry. "Don't be sad, mother," she would read. "I've had many joys, and I will have more. Where I am, life flows without spite and rivers never rush to find the ocean. You see, it can be done that way."

Clutching his guitar, the man walked away into the cloud-covered night, and the earth glowed under his feet.

Whirl of Birds

Turn the wheel, flow with the road. Pass houses, businesses, cars. In the weightless Texas air, everything flows by as a fragmentary landscape, luminous as the air breathing out of her body. Sinuous, the road, like the touch of his fingers blindly tracing her lines.

The sensation still in her pores, still feeling his face on her face, Bianca turns the wheel and turns the wheel. The car is taking her home instinctively, like a horse. Her body is still somewhere else, bending with his body of seething muscle, inebriation of Sam, only Sam. She can still feel the sheets on his bed, where she's left her phantom burning, inhaling burning air through her own strands of yellow hair in motion.

The car slows down quickly, as if by virtue of some metallic instinct. Bianca barely notices. She is aware that the car is no longer moving, yet feels nothing in her numb toes but that mad rhythm of perishing endlessly, skin to skin, without bones and without thought.

Her eyes fly above the traffic lights, pulled up by the force of the blue vastness, and she sees birds.

Black birds fly in circles, slow to the human eye, swirling in a dance they know as precisely as they know the winds and the prey. Long winged birds—vultures, maybe, or buzzards. Her mind sobers in slow fractions of a second. She wonders what they are doing right there, above the roads of a busy town—twenty of them, perhaps. Waves of Sam seep out of her body and she resents that, looking up at the birds that dance above the moments she cannot keep. In just another microsecond she knows the light will turn green, but the microsecond lasts longer than that. More birds gather vertically: a lazy tornado of wings.

Green light. Her mind moves her foot from the break to the gas, her eyes lingering on the sky. For what unfathomable ritual have these birds gathered, and why does her soul feel suddenly depleted? The slow turn of the whirl of birds hypnotizes. There's a meaning up there, something that the sky wants her to know, something about the immortality of heights. She will tell Sam about it. One by one, the birds move from the whirl pattern to lines, like soldiers acquiring a new purpose.

She has to watch the traffic, but the mystery of the sky makes her eyes drift. She looks ahead, hoping for another red light so she can look up again. It is as if her soul is hungry for a secret, something to make her feel part of the flow of time. She stops at the light, opens the window and looks up. The birds are scattering in small files. She wonders what the earth looks like from that height. She wonders if the birds can laugh—or something ticking inside them can laugh. She sees herself, spectrally, at the beginning of the row of birds and at the end of it too. A thought from earlier that morning comes to her mind. Any life is made up of a single moment—Borges said that. She talked about it with Sam on their way to his house. She will soon be twenty, though she's always believed that to be a hundred years away.

Borges thought immortality belongs to creatures that are ignorant of death. These birds seem to know death, and they are flying to different corners of the world to disseminate that knowledge from above. You just don't have as long as you think, she concludes. Only Sam is a place with no death.

The loud crash wakes her from her reverie.

She hasn't been paying attention to turns and lights because of the birds. After drifting onto the curb, her car has hit a fire hydrant. She jerks forward, the seatbelt cutting into her chest. The car beeps. People stare. Can it be that her whole life is caught in this one moment? Her life has been spared, but can it end in just another second? Can she be following the last bird to eternity?

As Sam's name dissipated like fog, for a few seconds Bianca had no idea where she was. She waved that she was ok and put her car in reverse, hoping nobody was calling the police. She glanced at the crumpled nose of the car as she drove away from the scene of her crash.

Everything flooded her brain like exploding grenades. She tried to regain some semblance of lucidity: she was in a car, yes, but she was not sure why. She was driving on the street, but the street was foreign. Objects, businesses—she could recognize those somehow, yet it was as if she had suddenly appeared in that place after a hundred years. Nothing knew her anymore. People in other cars seemed to be as wrecked as the front of her car. Her hands clutched the wheel and she focused on getting home. Home was close. She made herself drive to her house.

The driveway sat under the handrails of a narrow terrace. She pressed the remote and drove into the garage. Resting the car in the center without even looking at the damage, she locked the door and came out remembering that her mother had told her to buy who knew what.

Amidst leafy trees and gated houses taller than hers, there was something sadly comforting about her house. The square walls of the two-story building stood benignly before her, yet her hand trembled when she unlocked the front door. There was a weight on her chest, and she searched for thoughts to reassure her.

She felt dusty, before she even opened the door. She stepped through the tall vault and into the wide living room. Specks of dust whirled briefly in the rays she had brought with her. The door closed and the air stood still. She felt as if she had done that before, she had seen that before, as if she had stepped into the house a hundred times before, to find that same disaster. Or maybe she had dreamed it a hundred times, in dreams with a sinking feeling. On the wall opposite the door, the fish tank was the wrong color: instead of clear-blue, the water was murky-green. An overwhelming guilt came before the thought, and she knew why there was no movement in the tank. Her fish were dead. She spotted the small bulging bodies on the surface of the water and wondered how many days they'd gone without food before they'd given up and died. Red neon corpses, orange clown corpses, and her favorite, the black orchid. Bubbles stuck to the bodies and to the algae. There was a mistake, somewhere. There had to be. Even the water smelled like dust.

She suddenly thought of the parakeets in the sunroom. Sam's gift to her. She rushed there, the dreaded image already in her mind, her mouth dry.

The two small birds lay at the bottom of the cage, withered in their feathers. Dry seed shells and dirt concealed the smell of shriveled bird flesh. The water was long gone. She covered her face, shaking her head with a mechanical no, no, no. She had to sit. How long had she not been home? How many things had she forgotten—what else had died?

She stumbled to the kitchen and pulled out a chair, resting her elbows on the dark table. The house had sunken in darkness. The kitchen was the only place where there was still daylight coming through the window. There was something she knew would bring back her smile, if only she could remember what it was.

The phone rang.

She jumped. That was precisely the smiling thing she'd been waiting for. This call, of all calls, would tell her what she could allow herself to hope for. She pictured her voice speeding through space like an airplane flying a million miles a minute, to greet the voice of the man who used to miss her even when he went to the store to get pasta and wine. From the other end of the world came a questioning hello.

"No, everything's fine," she said.

"Oh, you should have seen her face when I showed up at her door with your mom," she laughed. "I don't think she ever got over you—" She held her breath to hear the laughter on the other side. It sounded impotent, drowned in street noise.

"Can you cancel everything and come home, Andy?" she purred.

"I miss you more, Andy."

She said it again, to make it last.

Yet through all this, she could not, for the life of her, picture his face. His postcard in her hand, she tried to place him in front of a building, under a tree, inside a subway car. Nothing was ever fair. How long had it taken her to forget

Sam's face?

She dragged her feet to the roomy bathroom. She changed into her bathrobe and washed her face. Glancing in the mirror, she averted her eyes from the ever-multiplying gray hairs. After all, her children would soon be home from school. Silvia would call any minute to tell her she was on her way to picking them up.

Her bones creaked and ached, as if carrying someone else's weight. She never used to have panic attacks. Breathe, breathe, that was always the idea. Chest pain, temple pain, loin pain, heart pain, they always told you to breathe. It was the same with joy. Breathing was the way to everything, and it always ended by making the moments fade away. She breathed, sinking her nostrils into the plush sleeve, to make her breaths last. Her face was heavy in the darkness of cloth. Her breath no longer came from tree blossoms.

She tried to remember what had made her uneasy before. Uneasiness was hard to remember, the feeling always stronger than what had caused it. It was the feeling she used to get when a glass broke, or a fancy plate. Lost. Could not take care of it, could not keep it. She settled, with a grunt, on the living room couch and grabbed the remote. Good or bad, the news gave her the comfort of noise. The news showed the mugshots of an old married couple. Slightly disheveled, slightly puzzled. They had been caught after repeatedly stealing pudding. Chocolate pudding.

She smiled, thinking Steve, her husband, would be home soon. They'd laugh about the news together.

The feeling of uneasiness persisted, lodged in her chest. She could take a nap upstairs. And she could rinse the dusty taste out of her mouth.

On top of the stairs, the bathroom door opened before her, and she had not even touched the handle. A woman came out, a woman she did not know. She was short and naked, old as if time had forgotten her. A bulging stomach with dark spots and lumps of flesh with no purpose hung over gray legs that could not keep her straight. Frail breasts. Fat tissue and bones under translucent, rubbery skin. Her murky eyes looked nowhere.

The woman lifted her arm and pointed a gun straight between Bianca's eyes.

A rage as old as the woman's soul swelled into Bianca's throat, and she heard herself screaming. She grabbed the old woman's hand and shook it, with no regard for the gun pointed at her face. The hand went limp.

"This is *my* house!" she shouted. "This is *my* house, and you are not allowed! Why aren't you dead already!"

The gun dropped to the floor, yet the old woman looked at her as if the fight was far from over. The old hand, left with nothing to hold, slid down

Bianca's arm and grabbed her elbow with the strength of something hungry and mean.

The old woman grunted, pushing. A gust of wind opened the balcony door, and the white curtain flew toward them. The two women twirled in a waltz past the curtain and into the balcony, reaching toward each other's throat, a spectacle for the street.

Minutes and hours passed in the space of mere seconds.

"Die, witch!" Her words came out with venom.

She pushed the woman farther on the balcony, and they entangled their arms almost lovingly over the rails. The old fingers pulled Bianca's robe, uncovering her breasts. Bianca, feeling no shame, pushed harder and pried open the old fingers. She pushed again, and the ancient body bent over the black rails, shaking them furiously as she tried to hold on. The woman's legs flew over the metal bar, flesh jiggling. One frail hand still held on.

She fell like a sack, crumpling on the ground. Bianca stared, breathless. The woman below, in her bathrobe, was shuddering her last moments. When the dying face moved and the eyes looked up, Bianca saw her own face, the face of many years ago. Her own body. Bianca lifted her hand and looked at the shriveled skin. It was obvious who had won.

The face of the young, dying woman fluttered one more beautiful smile from below, remote and promising. Her eyes gripped Bianca's in a deathly stare, and her breath spread into the air one more time. She was still.

Her hands shaking on the rail, Bianca realized she was naked above the silent neighborhood. If only Steve could hurry his old bones. If only she could remember what she meant to tell him.

Leaving the balcony, a whisper of tires on pavement made her stop. He was home. Above, a bird was making slow circles, tracing an unseen tornado in its descent and bringing back a vague memory. She watched the bird, a big one, thinking it was there for the corpse. She hoped Steve would not trip over that dead girl.

As the bird drew closer, it stayed suspended in place a few seconds, then landed on the rail.

With a smile, Bianca retreated behind the curtain.

Mahogany

The entrance door closed with a wooden thump. He listened to the floor creak hastily, and soon his wife was in the studio.

"Al—"

"I know. It's eleven," he said.

"They're asleep." Her voice did not accuse. She looked around. "Working on some new pieces?"

"Yeah I am. The kids asked for me?"

"No, they just—They watched TV. They wouldn't shut up about some show. Something about Buddhist monks who make amazing paintings on rice, then destroy them. Crazy, isn't it?"

He looked away.

"I've heard of them."

She walked to him and closed the top button of his jacket.

"Soon you'll see your breath here." She pulled her own coat tighter around her body, with a small shudder. She saw his eyes resting on the large stain on her coat. "What, I don't wear this in town." She took a step backward.

"Careful."

A black hardwood mallet lay among the wood shavings, at her heels. She let out a small, emphatic breath through her nose:

"You could be more organized. Or you could let me put all these on the shelf."

"They are where I need them."

"On the floor?" Her eyes narrowed.

"On the floor."

She drew a long breath:

"It's cold as hell."

"I'm not cold."

"You should be."

He reached with his hand and grabbed the back of the only chair in the room. He leaned on it. It was a walnut chair—a comforting, streaked brown.

"Don't wait up for me. I'm not done. I won't wake them up, don't worry," he said.

"I understand it when you skip dinner with us, and they don't care. But you'll get dizzy again if you don't eat."

With her chin, she pointed at the wrapped sandwich on the table. He looked at it without interest.

"I'll eat it right now if it makes you happy."

"It's not about making me happy."

His eyes rested on hers for a second. He stepped to the table and took the sandwich. It rustled.

"How can you stay here without a fire?" She watched him chew, big mouthfuls, big gulps. "Do you know how cold it's gotten? It will be below freezing overnight. They said that."

"Yeah," he said, chewing still. "I'll make a fire at some point."

In the corner of the room, the metal stove looked abandoned.

"No, you finish eating. Where do you keep the wood again?" She looked around, and her eyes fell on the small stumps lined up by the wall.

His eyes grew wide:

"Are you crazy?"

"Relax, I know that's not the firewood. Is it in the closet?"

His eyes quickly turned to the door of the small closet, opposite the corner with the metal stove.

"It's not there. I just bring it from the pile outside. I don't keep any in the studio."

"Fine, fine, I'll get it," she said. "I wasn't going to burn your cherry woods, your—your mesquites, your whatevers, your basswoods. Not after you spend that kind of money on them."

"*Mo-ney.*"

"Yes Al, money. Money is real."

He looked down, his jaw tightening.

"Don't get upset now," she said. "I'll bring the firewood." She stepped carefully among gouges, chisels, and pieces of wood.

"I keep them where I need them, remember?" he said to the open door of the studio. Then he relaxed and sat on the chair, slumping. He looked at the closed closet door. Gaze fixed, he lifted his square chin slightly. His eyelids half covered the dilated pupils, and he drew a deep breath.

When she stepped back into the room, carrying a pile of wood, he straightened himself and looked at her:

"Thanks. Please don't mix those with my wood."

"I know, Al."

"You know."

"All these years, and you think I don't?"

She arranged the twigs and left breathing room for the fire. Then she put in the thicker wood. She groped behind the gray stove, finding the box of matches.

He walked to the window. Outside, the small path to the main house glittered in the night. A few moments later, she joined him, and her hand rested on his shoulder. He did not move.

"I feel as if you don't want me in the studio," she said. "There was a time when we would come here, to hide from the kids."

"Yes. But now you can see—"

"Sure. You have so much going on here. I'm just a pest." Her hand fell from his shoulder to her side.

"Oh, don't start with that." He took her hand and squeezed it slightly, and he let go just as fast.

"I like how you can always see when someone's coming from the house. Nobody can surprise you."

Still watching the house, he nodded.

She turned around. She looked at the various small tables, each with a different project on it. Abstract shapes on a twisted log with roots on it. Half of it human-looking. Small birds taking flight, encased in shapes that suggested cubes and spheres. A big bust carved in heavy, kiln-dried boards glued together.

She sighed.

"Are you seeing someone, Albert? I'm tired of asking, but are you?"

He looked at her, tilting his head backward. His upper lip lifted, vaguely revealing the white of front teeth. His eyes were filled with some kind of sorrow, like that of the branches that shook in the winter wind outside.

"Do you want me to stop working on my art? Is that what you want? This is the only thing I do outside the house. Do you ever see me going anywhere?"

"I do go to work, don't I? I don't know what you do—"

"My whole life is in here. And I don't hear you complaining about the money that comes of it."

"You have a life in the house, too. No need to shout." She reached for a chisel on the shelf. It had a wooden handle, darkened by use. She dropped it back absently, and it rolled for a second among other chisels.

He sighed:

"What do you want me to say, except I'm not cheating."

"You don't even touch me anymore. The kids have noticed."

He bent his head. With the tip of his shoe, he cleared a small space among the shavings, on the wooden floor.

"You just hate to see me work," he said through his teeth.

"Come on, you know I love your work. Ok?"

"Yeah."

She moved away with sudden cheerfulness, stepping close to look at a sculpture of twisted wooden flames. She caressed it with her fingers. It was red, a layer of wax polish making it shine under the two lamps.

"Is this the one you're closest to finishing?"

"Kind of." He smiled, pushing his weight away from the windowsill. "I guess it is."

"You said it's supposed to be a woman?"

"It's a dance. It's a woman dancing."

"Oh. It's beautiful. It will sell fast."

"Um-hm."

He let out a laugh, startling her.

"What's funny?"

"The life it will have," he said, "on someone else's shelf. That's what's funny. People will gawk at it when they visit, and someone will dust it once a week. Because whoever buys it will have dusting habits. Don't you see?"

"It's sad, it's not funny. You have no control over the life it will have in that house."

"Yes. It will be like an adopted child."

She wrapped her fingers around the red sculpture, protectively. She looked out the window, toward the house.

"I guess it must be like that to you," she said. "Maybe that's why those Buddhist monks destroy their work. Or is it because of their religion?"

He shrugged.

"Could be."

"Well, I better go back. I hope you won't be here all night."

"No. Maybe I'll just finish up this one."

When the door closed, he watched her back shuffling toward the house, smaller and smaller, and dark. He pulled down the blinds.

He went straight to the closet and opened the door. He bent, lifting a heavy object covered in a white sheet. He brought it to the only empty table, and he set it there with infinite care. His fingers trembled as he took off the sheet, like a dress. He smiled lovingly.

The sculpture was a woman. Her whole body, unclothed and unashamed, was soft with the red of warm mahogany. He'd made her of one large piece, the most expensive piece of wood in the studio. She sat with one leg tucked under her, leaning one elbow on the folded knee. The other leg hung over the table's edge, like a child's. Her stylized, unrealistically narrow back curved in a long serpentine to the right, smooth and serene like the water of lazy rivers. Her small hands half covered her round, hardwood breasts as she leaned forward with her head bent above the floor.

Her head was wild, oversized. It was how this obsession had started: that singular image of a girl bending over the counter, her hair falling carelessly around her head as she scribbled something on a piece of paper. He'd never seen the girl again after that, and he wasn't sure he'd even fully seen her face.

The mahogany woman looked down at him as he knelt in front of her. He searched for that perfect angle from which her body did not look out of proportion. She had the eyes of creatures of the woods, pure and shining without layers of polishing wax. He had smoothed her mahogany skin with his razor-sharp chisel, to take away the edges. He had rounded her curves with the sculptor's spoon. The fishtail had vanished any impurity, and his ferrule had made her skin glow. The sander had caressed her, the buffer had teased her, the oil had turned her lustful. His febrile fingers had reassured her he'd been there all along.

And now he was looking up at this piece of wood, this miracle. She bent toward him, pouring her love upon him, filling him from top to bottom with that unrestrained, untamed mahogany devotion, until his body began to shake. Not with cold, no. He could finally take his jacket off. And his sweater, and his shirt. His pants. He had to be as bare and honest before this creature of his soul, as she was before him.

He reached up with both hands. Her head was fragile between his trembling fingers, and she did not recoil from his touch. He traced the waves of her hair, the roundness of her cheek, the long, long neck. When his hand reached her curved back and felt its smoothness, his hand stopped, and he started crying. He cried with abandonment, never covering his eyes, so she could see him cry.

It was three in the morning when he was kneeling in front of the metal stove, and his hands entrusted her body to the fire. He watched the flames take her, consume her, love her in a way he simply could not. It was vital for him to say goodbye now, not later. Not even a day later.

No one would own her, tame her. Not even him.

He left the studio like a drunken man.

Driving with Sara

You see me standing by the tree. You ask me the time. I show you my watch, from my pocket. It doesn't have a band anymore, but it shows the time. I sit on the bench. It's warm outside. A seagull screams in the sun. The leaves throw little shadows on me. You look like a nice lady, and I like your hat. You can be my friend because you smile.

That's when I remember how I saw on that channel, on TV, the cheetah. Running, it was, running after the baby zebra, and I could see the fear in the eyes of the baby zebra. It could never outrun the slim, big cat that wanted to eat. But that was not the worst of it, no. The mother zebra, she was running alongside the cheetah, as if she could stop it. The mother was not afraid—she looked brave. That's why I turned the TV off right then, so she could stay brave forever. Then I started crying. I am crying now, on the bench, because I remember. You sit down with me.

"Are you all right?" you ask me.

"I'm just a little hungry," I say.

You bend to look at my face. I will not tell you about the zebra. I will let you think I am hungry and I will smile my old smile that I practiced in the mirror.

But that was before. That was how we met. It is different now, Sara. You stay right here, and you won't be cold. I can bring more blankets. Sit with me while I drive.

My daughter came to my house when the old cat was still alive.

"I will help you clean the house," my daughter said.

"You come on Saturday, and you help me clean," I said.

She looked at me the way she looks when she wants to be my mother.

"That's what you told me last week, and the week before," she said.

"This Saturday for sure." She didn't believe me. I could see it in the way she pursed her lips.

"I can only help you so much. You'll end up like grandpa," she said to me, but she didn't know. I was the one who picked him up every time, and he would piss in my car. I didn't notice the smell anymore. I made him laugh.

Then she came on Saturday and she had cleaning bottles and rags and she said she had a vacuum in the car.

"I have to go babysit your cousin's kids," I said. "You and Patricia grew up together. Remember?"

"You always have somewhere to go." She looked at me like she was going to pour Clorox all over me. "I'll start cleaning while you go babysit. It will take me days anyway." I think she was already yelling.

"I have to be here when you clean," I said to her. "I don't want you to throw my things away. Only I can tell you what you can throw away. I have to go through all the piles of old magazines first."

"But those piles cover the whole living room floor!"

"I have to pick through them. I'll look Sunday."

"Let me take those piles of clothes to the cleaner's, at least."

"I can't afford it."

"I'll help pay for it."

"No. You have plenty to spend on, what with the baby coming. I'll just sort through the piles and take some to the Salvation Army."

She wanted to take away my things. Everything, if she could. She grew up in this house, and she forgot how she used to play with those toys from the back room. I remember.

"I can't take this anymore, Mom." That's what she said to me. "I love you, but I can't come to your house anymore. You know you can come to our house whenever you want, but I can't come here anymore if you don't let me clean. I don't even have a place to sit."

Later, they made me take the cat to euthanize her. I tried to save her. She breathed hard and growled for three nights and three days and then I wanted her to die peacefully but I could not see her put to sleep. It was expensive too. This old cat, she used to eat bananas, can you believe that? But then she could not use her teeth and she could not walk anymore. Then she would not stop growling and she couldn't even move. I could not stop crying. They made me take her to where she could die.

But that was before, when my daughter was still married. Then she moved into my house, and I was scared of what could become of us. I couldn't wait around to see what she would do to the place. We were screaming at each other a lot. I made it so she wouldn't find me. I said I was living with my aunt, but my car was my home. That was when we met, Sara.

I still think of the people I used to visit. Like her cousin and her daughters, and how we used to laugh so hard when I babysat them. My friend from the real estate job, and her little boy. Sometimes I was the only one who could get him from under the table. I think of them when I sleep on the beach, how I would like to make sandcastles for them. It's pretty here, with palm trees. I didn't grow up with palm trees. I was good in school and I got a good job. I was good at selling those houses back then, to the families with kids who go surfing and chasing girls with perfect bodies.

Why, no sir, I could not smell that smell you say. I didn't know she was in my car.

I know her, yes. Her name is Sara.

I met her on the beach. She was looking in the garbage. Or was it in the park, where the benches are. Sometimes we both slept on the benches. She has family somewhere. Not in California. Somewhere cold. It can get cold here too.

Sir, I did not know she was dead. She's like a daughter to me.

Yes, she was really thin. I think she didn't like to eat. She looked in the garbage for cigarettes, mostly. And booze bottles with a little left inside. I didn't tell my daughter about her, because she would think I wanted to scare the baby. But she is not a bad person.

I think I said all these things to the officer, Sara, and he will not leave. The officer blinks many times, dropping his jaw like a Muppet.

"Carl, come see," he says to the little black box in his hand. "Ma'am," he says, "why did you leave your car parked illegally?"—"Ma'am, you cannot deny there's a smell in your vehicle."—"Ma'am, you cannot deny there's a dead person in your vehicle."—"Ma'am—"

He Ma'ams me a lot, and I don't like it.

"I was paying for the gas," I say to him. "I was returning in a minute."

"Ma'am, are you aware of your surroundings?" he asks me.

"I am aware. This is close to the gas station."

"This is a fire hydrant and the gas station is on the other side of the road, Ma'am."

"She was my friend," I tell him.

"So you do know the dead person in your vehicle. Did you put the blankets on top of her?"

"Yes sir."

"Did you drive around with a dead woman in the passenger seat?"

He writes things down and I am not happy. I knew this was going to happen. I knew I shouldn't tell anyone about my friend.

"Ma'am, how could you not smell this? A box of baking soda in your car does not cover the smell."

"I have an old father. I'm used to smells."

The other officer comes, and he calls another officer. More of them arrive. I do not like this. I do not like this at all. She was my friend.

"I let her sleep in my car when it got cold at night."

"And you're aware she died. What did she die of?"

"She was thin. I tried to save her."

"Can you tell me how long she has been in your vehicle?"

"A few days."

"Look at this, Carl. It's a mummy. It must've been months. Have you kept her here for months, Ma'am?"

"Yes."

"Are these your coats on top of her?"

"Yes."

I say yes now. I want them to leave me alone. He takes me to his car, and there are seagulls screaming above. This time of day there will be surfers. I heard of a shark as big as a bus, lives in the water. I saw it on TV. It's called a megalodon. The surfers aren't scared, so I don't need to save them.

"My daughter. I need to call my daughter. She will know what to do. I need to go home."

The Return

"Melvin, they said someone's waiting for you," the secretary said. At the same time, she was nodding encouragingly, for him to continue.

"Give me one minute." Melvin leaned loosely on the glass of the secretary's booth, his arm pliant like dough under the pressure of his large body. "You see, frogs just can't throw up. If something is so bad in their stomach that their retching reflex gets activated, they will vomit their whole stomachs out."

"That's horrible, Melvin! Do they die?" The voice of the financial assistant came from the office's open door.

"Leave him alone," the secretary shouted toward the hallway. "He makes it sound fascinating. So, Melvin, you were telling me about those temples, where they worship the rats."

"It's not worship, really. They pay their respect to the rats. There are tens of thousands of them in some temples, and you'd be surprised how big they grow. People come from far away to see them, and they believe the rats are just waiting to reincarnate as people. They're treated like royalty. I'm sure you'd get used to rats if that was your culture, Shirley."

"You give me too much credit." The middle-aged secretary twirled her hair. "I'm not that open minded."

"You give people a chance, they get used to anything," he said. "You don't give people a chance, they wither. Am I right? Did you know that rats can have nervous breakdowns if they're left without their packs? And we think we're the only social creatures. You know what I mean?" His eyes wrinkled slightly as he smiled.

That was Melvin's signature smile. It made his broad face even broader, like a benevolent moon-creature, a beardless, giant gnome. Whenever he smiled, he looked fully in the eyes of the beneficiary, as if to press that goodwill past the surface until a smile came back in response.

Melvin wore his hair in a ponytail, quite long for all the formality of his job, yet never greasy or breaking loose. The shirts he wore were a different color every day, though there was no pattern in the repetitions. Coworkers at the company liked the unpredictable nature of the colors, and loved to speculate: will it be lilac today? Will it be gray because it's raining?

His boss used to be happy about his dexterity with numbers and allocation tables. Error resolution was once Melvin's forte, and his export files used to be impeccable. After a series of personal dramas, coupled with getting older, his mind wasn't as sharp as it had once been. While his smile had grown bigger with the years, sadder in its earnestness, it did not compensate for his forgetfulness. Numbers no longer fell in place for him, and it became clear after a while that he could no longer work as a financial analyst. Yet, he was not laid off: he was just made assistant to the financial analyst. Mostly, people liked to have him around. He was the kindest soul.

In the lobby, the thin, thirty-ish woman looked at her watch. She had been waiting for a good ten minutes, trying not to attract too much attention as she sat on the hard chair. Pale-faced and dark-haired, she turned her head many times to look at people coming in or going out of doors. She smoothed her skirt and gripped her knees with her hands. The clerk smiled at her.

When he came into the waiting room, Melvin was still laughing, saying something to those behind him about the number of vertebrae in the giraffe's neck. The laughter dwindled to a stop as he saw who was waiting for him. He stood in the dividing door for a few seconds, the smile—now a grimace— slowly receding. He stepped toward her, then stopped again. He touched his forehead, pointed a finger at her, then his fingers retreated into a timid fist that he hid in his pocket.

"It's good to see you," he finally said. Another waiting woman and the receptionist looked away, but their faces had the awkward immobility of discreet intrigue.

"Hi, Dad." The thin woman stood up, moving as if to hug him, but she didn't.

"Let's talk in my office," he said. His broad smile came back. "But I'm terribly busy, Ella, I'm afraid it has to be a short visit."

She followed him quietly, not really trying to keep up with his large steps. She nodded at people. Right before reaching his office, he turned his head to whisper to her: "My office may not be safe. It could be bugged." She lowered her eyes to the floor.

As they came into his small, starkly decorated office, Ella sat down on the leather-covered bench. She looked at the windowscape darkened by rain clouds. Her father sat across from her, at his desk, and leaned over.

"So Ella, baby, why did you come here? It's against company policy, you know that."

As her eyes fell on the large man, framed by the window, they lost the shadow of the clouds she'd been looking at. They sharpened, turned greener.

"I wouldn't have, if you'd only returned my calls," she said.

"I don't like *phones*, Ella," he whispered. "You never know who's listening."

She rolled her eyes and looked out the window again. He changed his position.

"Baby, you really *are* worried about me?" he asked.

She sighed, her eyes returning on him, softer now.

"I'm always worried, Dad."

"You know I get by," he said, playing with a pen on the desk. "I've been fine. I just get so busy, you know."

"Why won't you talk to me?" she asked, lowering her voice to a whisper. Her hands retained an imperceptible shaking. "I'm still your *daughter,* right?"

"A daughter over the phone?"

"Do I have a choice besides the phone? I would come over—I mean, you know I'd come over but I can't— And *you* said I shouldn't."

"No, you shouldn't be in that house. It would just—It would make it worse. It would be giving you ideas again." He watched her, as if looking for a trace of denial in her eyes. The frail woman seemed to be shivering. He cleared his voice as she looked away. "But I'll visit you more often. How is that?"

"More often than once or twice a year?"

"Well… It's easy to lose track of time."

Her eyes fell to the level of his hands. "Dad?"

"Yes, baby."

"Why are you wearing gloves?"

He laughed. She did not laugh with him.

"I'm allergic to fresh ink." Beads of sweat were forming on his face.

"Dad, you're not depressed, are you? Are you depressed again?"

"Oh, come on, Ella. It's been years now. I've been—I've been seeing some ladies."

Her pale face briefly lit up, a vague smile brushing her face.

"I told you, I have a life," he said. "If you don't trust me, ask around. See for yourself."

"And you're not afraid I might actually do that?"

He pressed his wrist with his gloved hand.

"You just wanted to see me then?" he said.

"Obviously. You don't call, you don't answer my calls or messages. I thought maybe you needed to see your therapist again and you didn't want to."

"Baby, I'm *happy.* I have friends from work visit me. And I have lady friends. I've been managing great with the house and all."

"I can *try* to make myself go see you there," she said, her face darkening.

"No, don't come. It will make you run away again."

She gathered her shoulders in.

"Dad, I've seen therapists too. I'm much better, just so you know. Why won't you sell the house and move out of there? There's just too much in that house. Have you even taken down the pictures, put them all away?"

He looked at her blankly. Then his broad smile returned:

"Of course, I took a few down, in the living room. I only kept the ones upstairs."

"So you never take your—lady friends into your bedroom?"

"Actually, no. Why would you ask such questions, Ella?"

"Give me one example of a lady friend you say you have. You've been on an actual date? She's come to your actual house?"

"Sofia, a nice—veterinarian."

"And that's not a lie? Just tell me, have you even bought a new washer and drier?"

"Of course I did. All these years, what do you think?"

"You should have let me buy them for you. Now I'll have to come over to see if you're telling me the truth."

He looked at her with narrow eyes, sighing. His eyes dropped to his watch.

"Ella, honestly, I'm doing great. And you can't stay here any longer. Let's have breakfast tomorrow, okay? Or dinner. How's dinner? We'll catch up and all."

"Sure, dad. I'd love that."

He stood up, relieved. For the first time since they'd started talking, he managed to look paternal. He opened his arms wide. She hugged him, her face pressing against his shoulder. She patted his shaven cheek, her palm resting there a while. Her eyes were filling with sadness, so she turned around to leave.

"Answer the phone tonight," she said and closed the door behind her.

She came out of the building. She walked fast, with purpose. Her black strands flew in all directions and she winced from the cold city wind. She checked the meter and got into her car, shaking her head.

"You wish I'd call first," Ella muttered under her breath. She took a key out of her pocket, an old key. She stared at it for a moment as one would at an old friend turned enemy. With quick, angry moves she attached it to the key ring, and started the car. She had not used the key in four years.

Late that evening, Ella drove to his street, and parked two houses away from his. Walking silently, trying not to let her heels make much noise, she reached the cement path where tufts of grass were now growing from the cracks. She climbed the two steps to the door and stopped. She put her hand on her chest and breathed, then stepped away from the door. She looked down, clenching her teeth. She stepped up again, lifted her finger to the doorbell, and kept it in the air a few seconds. Her arm dropped to her side. She wiped a tear and quickly took out her keys. She pushed the old key into the lock and turned it. It worked. Yet she did not push the door open. She waited a few more seconds, then rang the bell.

There was some commotion deep in the house. Waiting, she kept her breath slow and quiet. No one opened the door. She knocked, rang the bell again.

"Dad, are you there?" she said, leaning toward the door.

She looked around for a few moments, and finally stepped down and went to the window.

It was hard to see through the blinds, but they were not completely tight against the light, so she could make out some shadows. One shadow, tall and moving. There were mounds in the room, of clothes, maybe. Then the shadow moved, or something about it moved. The mounds moved too. Small shades of darkness burst around the bigger shadow, and Ella jumped back, afraid to think what it was she was seeing.

She remained at the window awhile, aware that she was being watched. There were noises she could not understand, and she started to cry like she'd used to, long ago, when her father would be late from work and she'd think he was dead. That same feeling returned, that her father may die on his way home, may never reach the steps to the front door. It was as if all the years in between, with the loss they'd brought, had never really happened. She could not tell what was worse: that fear she had lived with, as a child, of losing her parents when one of them stormed out after a shouting match, or the loss that really happened, with the precision of a trigger, the one she could not wish away by burying her face in the pillow. Hiding her fists inside her sleeves, she looked at the window and felt, as vividly as long ago, that her father would never make it home. She turned and ran to the car.

She didn't call him. She let two days go by, and she came back to the house in the morning, before she had to get to work, knowing he had to be home, still. She parked a few houses away from his—and waited.

The house was silent, like the other houses. Then the garage door opened and her father came out. She lowered herself behind the wheel, straining to see. Objects were amorphous in the garage, but from what she could tell this wasn't where he kept his car. It looked like a room. It even had a table with a chair. There were clothes hanging in rows, on a wire. Ella's hands shook on the wheel, and she looked at the key on the keychain. She turned on the engine and drove slowly to the house.

Her father saw the car and rushed out of the garage, blocking her way so she would not get into the driveway. Ella had to stop abruptly. She opened the car door. The big man pushed it with his hands. Little muffled screams came from inside the car, like those of the little girl he'd once locked in the storage room because she went biking without permission.

She rolled down the window, trembling.

He was panting, his face drenched in sweat. His ponytail was loose and sticking to his face.

"I don't even… recognize you!" his daughter yelled. "How can you—"

"Shh, baby, it's all right."

"It's not all right. It was *never* all right when you said it was all right! Say something else to me, something that makes sense, or there will be no reason left for me to talk to you!"

He wiped his forehead with the back of his hand.

"Ella. Just think of what you're saying. *You* left this house," he said, his voice low. "*You* left me here. Now I don't want you to come here. I beg you, don't come here."

She looked at him, shaking her head desperately.

"You have rashes on your hands!"

"What?" He hid his hands around his back.

"What? What? Dad, you're sick! You're so sick you don't even know you're sick anymore."

He stepped away from the car.

"Please, baby, go away. Go away now."

"I can't give up on you." Sobs were shaking her small body. "But—" She looked at him with new anger in her eyes. "But I can see why *she* did. You just don't get it. It wasn't fair to me when she put that gun to her head, was it? Or did you think the world was made just for the two of you, *Dad*?"

He turned around and went into the garage, his head bent, his whole body bent as if he'd aged two hundred years.

It was late that evening when she came back. She did not hesitate to go up the steps this time. She went straight to the door, put the key right into the lock, and turned it. She pushed the door wide open.

Neighbors inside their houses would have heard the scream. Screaming still, she stood in the door, unable to look away from the middle of the living room. The memory of the small gun with the ivory handle flashed before her eyes for less than a second, as she looked at the carpet. The painful remembrance was swept away by the sight in front of her, by what was left of the living room. In the very spot where her mother had fallen long ago, her father lay now, flat on the floor. He lay on the old, red carpet covered in strange droppings and food, and a pile—a hellish mound of gray and white rats—were swarming all over the man's body. There were rats on the carpet, startled, scurrying with both slushy and squeaky noises to and away from her father's body, while more rats were climbing on the table, the stairs, and virtually every space that was available to climb. The living room was unrecognizable, and the dreaded image of her parents wrestling for the gun vanished under the piles of new and aging clutter.

Ella looked around without comprehension, as if she'd just woken up. She noticed that her now prone father was watching her, his eyes even more startled than hers. A rat ran over her foot and she jumped in place, backing up and almost losing her balance before she found the door. She slammed it behind her.

Her father stood watching her from the window, as she ran to her car.

"Baby," he said quietly, pleadingly.

She did not call for more than a week. Even looking at the phone made her cry, powerless to erase the image of her father among the rats. The phone did not ring. It did not ring, that is, until the following Friday when someone from his work who'd found her number asked her if she knew why he hadn't been there in days.

Ella could not go back to the house alone. With enough probable cause for a search warrant, the police allowed her to come along.

She stood in front of the same door again, and she did not know if she would be able to step inside. With her hand on her chest, she pushed back the pounding of her heart. The officers called for her father, and when they did not get a response, they opened the door with the daughter's key.

Ella held her breath. She let the officers go inside and find what they were meant to find. Would she feel immense pain, or immense relief if the whisper of that moment was telling her the truth?

A middle-aged woman with a ready face, whose tag said Officer Garner, stepped among rats and rat excrement without as much as a wince. She turned to the door:

"Miss Evans, please don't come in. I will come back outside to take you to your car. Officer Kalb, will you begin recording? I'll join you afterward."

The man in uniform stepped in, speaking into his recorder.

"We are observing a body," he said, "a dead body among what appears to be a swarm of rats—anywhere between seven to fifteen hundred visible rats. Some are pet store rats, some look like the wild kind. Note the ammonia smell, indicative of an accumulation of animal waste." He stopped only to lift the camera that rested on his chest, and he took a picture. "Note a few carcasses of rats at the closet door. Note the maggots on the rats. Probably dead long before the man died. I am drawing closer to the body. Note the empty bags of rat food. There may be rat nests in the mounds of dirty laundry. Rats are going underneath. There are many piles of household objects and some unidentifiable items." He took out a small camera, looking at the door again. "I am with the body now. Cause of death unknown, but there are no visible gun wounds, or signs of struggle. Only rat bites, though they appear to have been made posthumously. The rats were probably hungry."

When Officer Garner returned, she started taking the pictures. Pictures of massive heaps of plastic containers, milk cartons, rotting paper bags and chair carcasses. Pictures of rats nesting in clothes so old that they stuck to the floor. Old appliances, serving as nests. Soiled magazines and shoes with the leather gone, gnawed off. Holes in every wall. Scared creatures with beady eyes, waiting for order to be restored.

And in a cleared up space in the corner—a sweater, faded green, spread on the floor like a rug. In the middle of it, a phone.

The officers continued their recording. From the outside, nobody could see Ella in her car, for she had collapsed onto the passenger seat.

The officers did not record that the little animals nibbling at the man's flesh were joyful, not sad. That was to be the rats' last declaration of their worship and love, as they accepted his—for only gods and lovers will give their bodies so completely, unquestioningly, returning it to that source where everything *life* comes from, in endless, organic flows.

The cause of death was to be officially established as rat fever.

She could not have known that he had often talked to the ringing phone, without picking up, knowing she was at the other end. Yet for some reason she could not explain, the last time she went to the empty house, long after she buried him, she took the phone with her. It was a small comfort, looking at it sometimes, as if his voice would reach her from beyond the grave.

If I could talk to you, Ella, I would tell you that it all started with seven rats from the pet store. It was an idea the therapist planted in my mind: that it would be good for me to give care to something outside myself, since I was so bad at giving myself that care. She wanted me to have a link to the outside world, or else I'd withdraw even further into my torment. She said a small soul to care for would draw me out, and I'd eventually reconnect with you, my baby daughter, since I did so wrong by you after your mother died. The therapist said that before I could be a father to you again, I should start small: a fish, a bird. I chose rats, because they seemed playful at the pet store. Manageable.

Then, unnoticeably, it turned into love.

If you could only see how a mother carries her tail in her mouth, to her nest, before she has babies. She nurtures herself, like a pup, so she can nurture her own babies better. How can I turn back time and tell your mother that she did not love herself enough to be a good mother? I watched these small wonders, thousands of them as they went from birth to death with so much heart, you wouldn't believe it. Other females will help a mother raise a litter, and sometimes a male will help. Only a few mothers will eat their own, if something close to tragic happens to them. If their mate was killed by an aggressive male, if the food was scarce for a while, or if they were hit before giving birth. But even if she can eat her own babies, a mother rat will never take her own life. Do you see, my baby, why it is good to watch the small world before you can live in the big one?

Why, Ella, how could you ever think that I was to blame for her pulling that trigger?

I'd tell you something funny, if I could: I've learned all their chirps, their peeps, their squeaks and their squeals. I can call them to me, like that. Do you hear me? I am one of them. They tell me that when they chatter their teeth in my ear, like purring, and their eyes bulge with relaxation.

Rats are brave. They will fight for a female, and they will not stop when the rival rolls on his back. But fights aren't always doom and gloom. Sometimes they fight right on top of me, like children. They will end by licking each other, and they will lick me too. They like the salt on my skin. I like the purity of their small tokens of love. I'm just a big rat to them.

I've learned to love so I can love you again. Let my love be what you remember.

Painted Snails

Just as quickly as a whisper of wind, it became too late.

Poppa used to say it's never too late for revenge. Maybe that was why he drank himself to death before he could give someone what was coming. Maybe to his factory bosses, or the families in those big houses, five streets from ours, whose children went to school in cars—to a school so remote and mysterious that it might as well have been on the moon. Seeing Poppa stupor himself with cloudy bottles for the two hours a day he was near us, I swore I'd never be like him.

I wanted my revenge bright and early. I plotted it with my morning milk, when there was milk at the table, and I knifed my bread like the world was flattened on it, mired in jam, for me to step on. Sandy, my sister across the table, would startle to see my hands move, and she only jellied her bread after I was done doing mine.

The first and the last of my dreams of revenge was Angela. For some reason, even if she was barely better off than we were, it was easier to hate her than the distant rich. After all, did she not wear on her face the clean confidence of those other faces, of the girls peering from the windows of polished cars while we walked to our crumbling school?

Our parents and Angela's parents were chanting their laments at the brink of the Depression. Yet for Angela it was as if she already could see herself past poverty, ordering others around. She trained herself on us—on Sandy and me.

She told us to steal our mother's shoes and purse, to play at ladies on the sidewalk. Sandy accepted, with that tremulous eagerness to please her friend, only because Angela had upgraded her to "the sister she'd never had." Sandy had asked her, "Is Brenda your sister too?" Angela had grinned, snatching from my hands the doll she'd given Sandy, and had said—to the air, to neither of us—"I will decide when and where I make Brenda my sister."

It was her charm alone that brought the man with the monkey and the camera to take a picture of us in the street that day, with Angela in the middle. He said if we wanted the monkey in the picture, we'd have to pay.

She laughed at us for wobbling in our mother's shoes, her laugh knowing we'd be spanked later for dirtying and scratching those shoes, and we'd spend hours polishing them—not because they needed or could even take that much polish, but to learn. To learn.

I learned to be hidden, spiteful. I learned to let Sandy take all the scoldings, too scared of my proclaimed vengeful soul to tell on me. She would later tell about it to Angela, when they whispered and I pretended not to hear.

It wasn't too late for my revenge the time when Angela had us all paint snails with her mother's nail polish. She never got beaten for using her mother's things, so my heart was not in it. The snails were all alive in their shells, and when we released them in the grass, in the fenceless yard with the burned house, the snails carried away flowers, crooked horses, and names like Princess (that was Angela's), Bon-Bon, Curly. I planned to return to find the Princess snail and crush it. In the two days that passed before I could steal away from chores, the snails had all retreated in the impenetrable tangle of plants around the burned house. We would return to that yard later, to scare each other with dusk-tinged stories of people rotting among the ruins.

When Angela's father got a better job at the factory, and Poppa lost his to drinking, it was clear she'd be the one I'd have to hate forever. She was the first of us three to have a sweetheart—Gabriel. I was nice to him. I thought it would be enough to cross my legs in a way I had seen in movies, and he'd leave Angela for me. I would say things to him like "I can make cake," or, "My uncle will help me be a secretary," and "A palm reader said I'll have five children." I wanted those words to paint a story for him, where I'd love him and give him food and children. I never spoke ill of Angela, but he always watched me with suspicion when Sandy and I joined them in the park.

He did not marry Angela. He married my sister—though that was later, when he moved to California. I never sent him the bitter letter it took me two years to compose.

It wasn't too late for revenge even when Angela learned to pilot a plane— or so she claimed. Cory, her fiancé, was a pilot. Angela didn't take Sandy and me along when she went to see him. Just as the war started, she made herself a military wife. She carried that glow with her at the factory, where we all worked now. Sandy helped her write letters to the front. Around that time, I slapped my sister's face, not because I saw her kissing Gabriel, but because she seemed so grateful to Angela for not hating her. I wondered if they somehow shared both of those men, Gabriel the farm boy and Cory the pilot.

We survived the war—making uniforms and rucksacks for the soldiers. But even when Cory was killed somewhere in Europe, somewhere as cold and barren as his letters, I still could not feel sorry for Angela. I was long past the desire to be her sister.

No, I did not want to be her sister, because I would have had to pretend there was more than mutual interest when we left our children in each other's house, or when we went to fetch our husbands from the local bar. We compared the letters we got from Sandy, and I looked for jealousy in her eyes when she saw my sister had sent me the saddest parts of her life. The fake-bright parts filled her letters to Angela.

All those years with all the suffering, and the death of one of my children did not bring us much closer. It was still not too late for me to be the better one. For me to know the better people, raise the better children. I raced against the odds—and so did she—though I could not help but notice the ease with which she accepted the wrinkles, the fat that slowed her down, and the changing face of our little Iowa town. Keeping up with her, I was always one step behind.

Wisdom was also late to reach me. Only when I put the first flowers on her grave did I understand how much she'd been part of my inner landscape, how generous a part of all I had called happiness. When trees bloomed and snails bathed in the dew around her tombstone, that was when I finally grasped that wisdom.

Angela, my sister, *now* it is too late.

What Lingers

The leaves of Lehigh Valley were turning, trails slippery. Alex conceded silently that Dave had been right: one, the Susie situation was distracting him and two, they shouldn't have taken the most difficult trail out of Jim Thorpe. He felt the front wheel of his bicycle hit the boulder and he lost his grip of the handle. He imagined Susie laughing. The last thing she'd said to him was to marry his bike. Her face was still lodged solidly in those spaces of his mind that he could not fill with any other thought.

Maybe he had even closed his eyes before the bike hit the boulder.

He was rolling downhill, hitting rocks, too fast to register the hurt. He just knew bones and skin were rapidly snapping open, though life did not flash before his eyes. All he could think of was, this is bad, this is really bad. When trees and sky stopped switching places, his body rested on grass, and he saw water. Pain shot through his legs.

He convinced himself it was vital to remain aware of his surroundings, so he stared at the trees until they started to move. The trees turned into people. They were running back and forth, and their steps resounded on the cement floor. He could hear terrified voices.

Alex jumped to his feet. Nothing hurt, nothing was broken. His arms and legs were seeping adrenaline, and his neck was tight. The air was hot and bristly, and it was dark in the reactor room. His face hurt as if thousands of needles pushed against the skin from inside. He thought vaguely, I didn't realize you can *feel* the radiation. An enormous, ungraspable thought hovered above his eyes: lives, many lives depended on him. "Where is that Dave," he mumbled. "Dave," he let out a raspy shout. Without Dave, it would be hard to open both valves, yet the seconds ticked faster than the speed of fusion. There was enough steam in his lungs to cause a burst of blood and fear. The steam in the bubbler pool could cause a megaton explosion if the water wasn't drained before the corium reached it. Tongues of black corium flowed like lava with implacable precision, faster than he could shout for Valeri in the dark. He ran—almost floated to the water and dove in.

There was a muddy light somewhere in front of him—he was not alone in the water. Someone else was already turning a valve. That was Valeri. Alexei parted the murky water with his arms, barely seeing more than his own sleeves suspended like algae. Then the light was extinguished, and he had to remember where he had seen the other valve. He reached blindly, like a mole. The air in his lungs was long gone—perhaps he had drawn in no air when he'd dived, just corium fumes. The valve rumbled with the sound of sinking submarines, yet it turned, and the sluice gates opened. The water around him rushed past in waves, leaving him in the dark. He crawled, steaming, out of the concrete grave.

Everyone cheered. Their cheers stung, poisoned with enough radiation to kill them, and kill thousands more.

Later, Alexei Ananenko would die, and so would Valeri Bezpalov.

Alex opened his eyes again. His hurting legs were resting in the cold water of the river. No one was around. A sweet-scented fall wind stirred the red and yellow leaves in the thick branches. His head was pounding where he'd hit his head. His eyes blurred.

He adjusted his protective gear and pulled the big goggles over his face. The gear rustled on his body. He was one of the liquidators.

"Not your cat on the roof rescue," laughed another firefighter.

"We may rescue the cat, but we won't be around for the old lady to thank us," he grinned. That was easy, laughing in the face of death. There was no other choice but to take it easy, like a drill, and pump the cooling water among the chaos of shouts, the chaos of sand and lead and boron dropped from helicopters.

A brigade of young firefighters thought they were called to extinguish an electric fire. They did not know what graphite was, and they picked up hot pieces and marveled. Even seeing the devastation to the crumbled, smoking reactor, they did not know why their mouths tasted like metal, and why there was something deathly in the eyes of others. The young firefighters carried their hoses and ran to the place that others were running from. When darkness fell over the frenzy and brought with it the smells of great, smoking pits, the heaviness in people's voices grew.

The trucks the brigade had come with stayed parked in the same spot for over twenty years.

Heavily radioactive fires smoldered through the night, and in the days to come. Firefighters with scorched faces answered questions to foreign reporters, and a few weeks later, their bodies stopped fighting the poison and shut down.

Alex coughed out river water. Where is Dave, he thought.

One side of his face felt sticky, and he rubbed it. There was blood on his palm. Some part of his body must be hurt, he assessed as he dragged himself out of the water. His eyes turned to the sky—a pure sky. This same sky had looked just as pure decades ago, when the forests had felt the poisoned breath of the Three Mile Island power plant.

The air around grew nebulous—evil, maybe. He saw movement from the corner of his eye, and as he lay on his back, wet in the grass, he turned his head to see who was coming.

It was someone, or rather, something between a grown child and a creature. Its rags hung about its body, useless. Its arms had the shape of bones, too long for a child's body. Its feet had twisted toes. The face of the child-creature was pained, but quiet. Its head was oversized and shaped like a skull-balloon.

The eyes did not accuse: they only blinked, half-open.

The child with a head like a balloon drew closer. Alex felt no fear, only an immense sadness, something deeper than the loss of leaves in the fall. The tall child-creature held something in his hand, and he wanted Alex to take it. Vizmy tse, vizmy tse, the child said, and somehow Alex understood that he was saying, take this. It was an apple with boils on it, an apple poisoned by the very tree in which it had grown.

Alex blinked, and the vision faded. Soldiers ran past him. A convoy of people came from behind, sullen, carrying very little. Most of them did not know they would get cancer and give birth to babies with the wrong shapes.

Their belongings would remain in the town of Pripyat, frozen like broken clocks.

The leaves of fall returned above him, soothing in their innocence. For a moment, the bulbous head of the child floated above him, and the eyes staring at him were his own eyes in plastic reflection. An oxygen mask went over his face. A face was bending over him from between the leaves—someone else's face. It was a beautiful woman, and her hand pressed the oxygen mask. She was an EMT, and there were tubes around. The ambulance shook him slightly as it passed trees and buildings.

"He's awake!" the woman said, turning to someone. When she looked back at him, her smile was soft like the autumn light. She took away the oxygen mask.

"Did I fall?" he asked, feeling stupid.

"Do you know what day it is?" she said, close to his face.

"I think it's Sunday. Is my bike ok?"

"You'll get it from the police station later," she said, pulling the yellow hair away from her face. Round and smooth face. Blue eyes pure as the sky.

"My friend Dave—where is he?"

"He'll be at the hospital later. You have a good friend."

He tried to smile and the dried blood pinched his face.

"Tell me your name," she said. "No, don't sit up."

"Yeah, first aid drill," he muttered, letting his head fall back. His head hurt. "My girlfriend Susie broke up with me. Tell me, what does a girl want to hear, to go back with a guy?"

She shook her head:

"Name."

"I'll tell you my name if your name is as pretty as you are." He finally managed to smile.

She looked as if she was going to roll her eyes.

"Katya," she said. "Now your name, or I'll write down that you're not coherent. They'll put you under."

"I like Katya. That sounds Slavic. You don't have much of an accent."

The oxygen mask went back on his face. Her firm hand rearranged his head, shaking the achy brain all around his skull.

"Ah!" he said, louder than he would have if she'd been a man. The corner of her mouth painted a vague smile.

"I'm Ukrainian," she said and turned to bring a syringe.

He pulled at the mask.

"Alex Bower." He spelled it too. "And how did you end up in Pennsylvania?"

"All right, kid, no more questions. You know, they'll make you take off that lip ring when you get to the hospital."

He laughed.

"Come on, tell me, when did you come to the States?"

"In '86, with my family. I was just a girl."

"No way! That's the year I was born. How weird is that."

Her face did not change.

"So you don't remember your home country much?" he continued.

She gave him a look as if she was angry, or sad, or both.

"I do."

"What, there's bad stuff? '86, that was communism."

She just looked at him.

"Ukraine?" he said.

"We're at the hospital," she announced. "It was nice meeting you, and don't bike in the rain again!"

She bent close to him to release a buckle. She smelled like autumn leaves and peppermint.

"Yeah, but—Ukraine is where Chernobyl was. With that freaky explosion at the nuclear plant, right?"

She gave him a fast look and her eyes changed color.

"Were you there? Were you close?" he said as the gurney slipped from the truck and onto the ramp.

A scared child surfaced in her eyes. Her head bent in an infinitesimal nod.

"That close?"

"We were evacuated," she said. His gurney went into a bright hall.

"I know my leg injury is nothing compared—"

No, that wouldn't work. He took a deep breath. He had to tell her.

"Katya, you have to believe me, I'm serious now. I had a dream when I was knocked out."

"We all have dreams," she said, turning to walk away. "Get better."

"Please, wait," he shouted after her. "Katya, the dream was about Ukraine. Will you come see me later?" He could not read an answer in her slightly bent shoulders as she turned around the corner.

The nurses and doctors took over.

He didn't expect her to come back at all, but he kept thinking about it through his knee surgery and sleeping spells. He counted two nights and two days—enough time for Dave and for his mother to come see him.

On the third day, Katya was at the door.

"Oh, hey! What do you know, the pretty nurse brought flowers to the wounded soldier!" he shouted, looking past his leg in traction.

"I didn't bring you flowers," she said, walking to the bed. "Alex, right?"

"Katya from Ukraine," he answered, pointing with fingers from both hands.

She sat on the chair, hands folded on her lap. Her eyes were serious, so he closed his and tried to remember. He had wanted her to come see him for something, and it wasn't to tell her how beautiful her hair was.

"I'm here because you wanted to ask me about Ukraine," she said. "You had a dream, you said. You're going to tell me that meeting me wasn't random, I think."

"That's right. Chernobyl," he answered. "That's what my dream was about. Like I knew I was going to meet you."

She watched him and her eyes were remote, though it looked as if she wanted to pay attention.

"I've been dreaming the same dream since I was a girl—just not as often anymore. I left my doll on the ground, in front of my house. It's probably still there. I dream of that." Her voice shook imperceptibly.

He closed his eyes, as if he could not look at her saying that.

"What was your dream?" she said, and her voice was open this time, warm. "Tell me what happened."

He looked again, and she was smiling.

"I was lying there by the river—"

"You were wet. You probably fell in the river."

"Yes. I was lying there hurting like crap, and I thought my name was not Alex but—Alexei or something. And I was under water, although I didn't remember getting in."

"Why would your name be Alexei?"

"Yeah, right? That's from your part of the world. So why do I have to meet a Ukrainian right after I have some weird-ass dream?" he said, a fraction of his eyes looking to see if she was offended. "You said you were evacuated."

She nodded:

"Three days later. They couldn't even be bothered to tell the population we were being poisoned by the air and the rain. It was kept secret. Only when Sweden noticed radiation all the way there, our government admitted it and started the evacuation."

His eyes rested on hers for a long moment, as if to see how deep the hurt still remained.

"Look," he said, "I don't know you, but there's something strange that happened to me there in the woods. And then you tell me you're from Ukraine."

"So what's the big deal with me being from Ukraine?"

"I had just broken up with my girlfriend," he said. "I didn't really care if I biked blindfolded and fell over the cliff. I hit my head, and it was all so unimportant—Susie, all that stuff. I saw things like I was someone else, from Ukraine. I know you don't believe me."

"What did you see?"

"There was a valve, at the reactor, that needed to be turned, and someone else was there with me. The graphite melted and people found smoldering graphite on the ground."

She was quiet, waiting.

"Anyway, I'm not crazy, I didn't just dream about nuclear physics. I'm a nuclear engineering major at Penn State, so I know some of these things. Before Chernobyl, we had an accident at Three Point Island, and it was contained before it became a Chernobyl. After '79, they really got this stuff in shape, the plant designs, the containment, the pressure relief valves, staff training. Tell me, what was wrong with your government, communism or not, that they didn't have all the safety features that were put in place in the US and Europe? I read about this stuff. There was a big flaw in the reactor. There was a gap of a minute between when a power grid would fail and when external power would take over to start the cooling system."

She looked at him and lifted a finger.

"What?"

"What they told us was not very technical," she said. "I don't understand how reactors work, but you can't explain in any technical terms the fear that paralyzes you when you leave your house forever. Or the perplexity of trying to picture with your mind the invisible poison you know is in the air."

"I'm sorry, I didn't mean to—You know, I was literally obsessed with Chernobyl some years back. But I never met an actual person who was there."

"Now you have."

"But how do you explain how we met?"

"I don't know," she said. "Radiation lingers, and I suppose it catches up."

"Did you have any effects?"

"I have thyroid problems. My mom gave birth to a baby without a spine. He died."

"Oh God."

How does one respond to that?

"Tell me, Alex, what did you hope I would say to you?"

"What do you mean?"

"From the beginning, I feel as if you've been hoping for some answer from me. Do you want me to tell you that you shouldn't be majoring in nuclear engineering? That the world is too obsessed with nuclear power, nukes, nuking, and they don't have a clue what it does to people?"

"Come on, I'm not in this because I worship it. It's precisely the safety aspect—"

"Maybe you want from me something to jumpstart your brain after your breakup? You want me to spell it out, that there is pain in this world bigger than losing your girlfriend?"

"I know that."

"But at this moment it doesn't matter much, does it? You wanted to bike off the cliff anyway."

"Is it beautiful in Ukraine?" he asked without blinking.

She laughed softly.

"You're a nice kid. Yes, it's beautiful there and I miss it sometimes. But you leave things behind."

He looked in those sky-blue eyes for a long moment. Something in her eyes came from far away and it made a tiny part of him shift slightly, just like fall makes a tree shift toward another kind of light.

"Thank you for saving my life," he said. "In the ambulance. I think you're a good EMT."

She smiled.

"You'll be back on your bike in no time."

"Yeah, I'll heal. That's easy. I probably need to work on making it back to reality. That's a bit harder."

She smiled and nodded.

"You know," she said, "there is something about love that is like radiation: there are things we don't see, or we don't pay attention to, until they explode. Love is invisible. You have to get away when it's poisoning you. Contain it, move on. A really nice girl will love you one day."

He laughed. She came to his bed, squeezed his hand.

"I'll see you around," she said. Then she was gone.

He looked out the window, where the fall sun was red with thoughts of evening. In that moment, it was easy to let the poison out.

Prodigal

His feet remembered the path, five years later. He had lived on top of rugged rocks, hiding in thorny bushes, his cheeks taking the shape of mossy stones at night, when he slept. For five years, he'd caught salmon with sticks he had sharpened, and he'd picked cold berries with grateful lips, directly off the branches. He'd even learned to like the taste of fat worms that he lifted from behind the tree bark. Year after year, he had let go of his hate of people, but only little by little, person by person. Still, some of the faces, hideous and distorted, had taken a long time to vanish into nothingness. Five years, and most of the hate was gone. When he had just a smidgen of it left, just enough, he woke up one morning and thought, "Today is the day."

He walked part of the way, and ran some more. It took him two days to arrive at the first signs of others—and he thought his dread would return. But it didn't. He laughed, in anticipation of the first "Hello," thinking of himself and how he looked, as if a mirror were standing in front of him in the grass. He laughed again, when he saw a house. Who would know him? What town was this? Would he remember how to speak? He knew his name. It was Thomas.

There weren't any people around, though he passed several houses. In the sun, Thomas saw chickens pecking at the ground, and a few lazy cats on benches and on old, forgotten swings. He reached a road, something with asphalt at least, and his feet started to hurt a little. Trained to hear sounds from afar, he lifted his head. He sniffed danger. It came from somewhere up the road, where houses were closer together and there even seemed to be a small public square, with a fire department in the middle. He started to walk on front lawns, close to the houses, to avoid being seen. Several cats followed him. They kept their distance, as if they didn't entirely trust him and his wild smells.

The noises in the small town square were increasing. It was a chorus of growlings, something like a threat of many voices that weren't even human. Thomas stopped behind a big tree, because now he could see what the noises meant. There was a man, sitting on the paved ground of the square, his hands tied behind his back and his legs wrapped in some sort of sack. A hoard of cats, a mass of hundreds of them surrounded the man, growling in unison. The man struggled, shook and twisted his body, trying to move away from the beasts. There were three human silhouettes, standing at a distance, at the farther end of the plaza. A woman, a man, and a smaller figure—a child or a shorter man. Their arms were crossed, and they did not move either to run away, or to do anything about the swarm of cats and the tied up man.

There was a scream—one of the cats screamed like a hysterical woman, and the rest followed. Thomas could not see exactly how the sea of cats moved—but it was fluid, in one single motion, as if on command. The animals were upon the roped unfortunate in a second, and the terrorized hollering of the human did not even lift itself above the feline screams, for it was weak and it quickly drowned. Thomas rushed forward, hoping he looked bigger with his wild beard. He flapped his arms and let out a shriek of his own. But as soon as he was close to the periphery of the hoard, a patch of moving bodies detached from the main mass and quickly moved in his direction. He faltered, looked around. Across the plaza, the three figures were standing like before, with their arms crossed.

Thomas took a step back, as the cats slowly advanced toward him. His instincts were sharp, from the five years he'd spent in the woods, but in all those years of living in nature he had not seen something so directly threatening to him, multiplied in the eyes, fixed on him, of so many animals. He'd seen bears, he'd seen boars. He'd outsmarted them all. But now, these cats were of one mind—and their collective hissing was meant for him only. There was something calm about them too, as if they knew, as they advanced in their stalking manner, close to the ground and with ears drawn back, that he would retreat. The other man was no longer screaming, and Thomas could not tell if the cats were eating him, or merely tearing his flesh apart.

Thomas ran in the opposite direction.

"This way, man!" he heard from one of the houses. "Quick, they're not looking anymore!"

The old instinct of following instructions kicked in. Thomas ran to the house, though he could see no one at the front door.

"Over here, on the side!" he heard again. There was a small entrance to a basement apartment, and that's where he was being called. Someone grabbed him at the door and pulled him into a moldy-smelling, small room lit by a flickering fluorescent light.

"What the fuck is going on?" Thomas said, with his voice in a higher register than he expected. He realized those were his first words back among humanity, but he couldn't change them now.

"What's wrong with you?" said the man who had brought him in. He was small and thin, unshaven. He was missing a tooth. The man sat on a dirty couch and his wife came into the room. Her face was square and rough, and her arms were hairy like a man's.

"Wrong with me?" said Thomas, choking incredulously.

"What were you charging at them cats for? Come from prison or something? Got a screw loose?" the man knocked on his own temple with a bent finger.

"What prison?"

"We're playing the game of questions now? Your clothes. Your beard. You look like they kept you in for some time."

"Who?"

"What do you mean who? Them cats."

The two men looked at each other with bewildered eyes. The wife banged some pots in the kitchen. Thomas pointed vaguely outside.

"What was going on there? A man was just killed."

"Yeah, that's right. He was executed. What, you've never seen an execution before? How long did they keep you in, man?"

"I wasn't in prison," he protested. "Execution by cats, you mean?"

"Damn right. What else?"

"*Cats?*"

"What, you lived in a cave for the past five years?" said the man, wiping sweat off his face.

"In fact, I did."

"You did. You might as well have. So you don't know what's going on?"

"I can't even begin to ask what's going on," he almost screamed now.

"Billy, tell him to stop shouting," the wife suddenly spoke from the kitchen. "They'll hear. We'll be done for."

"Who will hear?" said Thomas.

"The cats. Upstairs. Whole bunch of families of them live in the house. People live in basements, mostly. There are more of the cats anyway."

"No, no, no. Stop talking like that," said Thomas. "What in the bejesus are you saying to me?"

"Wherever you said you were for five years, then you don't know nothing of it?"

"Nothing."

Billy scratched his head and looked up, to find inspiration for how to trace back the history of it all.

"Wanna sit you down now," said Billy. "I'll tell you what you need to know. Care for some liquor? Got a little smuggled…"

"What, there's no liquor now?"

"Not enough people to make it."

"Where did they all go?"

Billy sighed. Thomas sat on a chair and the wife brought them shot glasses.

"It all started with a loophole in them laws. Seems like the cats found a way to say they were people too."

"Huh?"

"They got some law to show they deserve personhood rights, something like that."

"A cat is not a person."

"It ain't, but it's a legal kind of person. Some people started to ask for tax breaks for their cats, and insurance, and for tax purposing they made them into people. They got 'em into the Constitution and it started from there."

"But that doesn't mean cats *know* anything about rights?"

"Turns out it's not so hard to know. Once they got word of having some of them rights, they wanted more."

"How did they even *say* they wanted rights?" Thomas said. He remembered he had the shot glass. He practically threw the clear liquid down his throat.

"With these phones these days, touch screens and all, it wasn't hard." Billy spoke matter-of-factly. "And then the cats somehow got word that abortion is murder, and they made it apply to them, to the spaying and such. They made all that illegal."

Thomas felt his body tingle all over. Rage, fear, he didn't quite know.

"But it doesn't make sense," he said, looking down.

"At the time, it did. What do we know? We're simple people. Let them lawmakers make the laws." A glimpse of sadness flickered on Billy's face. He may have felt a little bad for being simple.

"How could people stand for that?" said Thomas, defeated. "I thought I was the crazy one, living in the woods. I turn my back a couple years, and you all let it go to hell?"

Billy grinned sheepishly.

"Like I said, how many people know enough about them laws to figure out the loopholes? There should've been a plug for them loopholes long time ago, but how can you go back on it when they made it into law?"

"But they're *cats*, for god's sake!"

"Nah, don't worry yourself." Billy grinned again, slapping Thomas on the knee. "You'll find a job, doing something. There's always work. See, my wife works as a nanny for some of 'em, for the cats. There's always new litters, so she won't lose her job—ever."

"But did you say there are few people left now? How is that possible?"

"There were... diseases. With cats having most of the insurance, we couldn't afford much treatment. And now, we don't get too many children neither."

"They force people to abort?"

"No, abortion is illegal. But once a child is born, the child loses personhood. They have to earn personhood now. If they don't, cats have the right to... well, to execute them."

Thomas opened his mouth and eyes wide.

"They *kill* the children?"

"Yep... But it was voted on. That's how come you can't go back on it. If you wanted to vote on it now, you'd never get it any other way, because now there's more cats than people."

"Why the children?" Thomas said, feeling stupid.

"The children don't do anything useful, most of'em."

"They're too young to 'do' things. How can a small child know how to do things?"

"When you have to, you wise up real fast, don't you? At least, some of'em do."

For some reason, the wife started laughing. She was watching TV, a sitcom with cats.

"What's that Red Whiskers said?" Billy asked, stretching his neck toward the other room.

"Did he get those kittens to school without Lil'Paw?"

"Shut up Billy!" his wife answered. "You don't watch half the time and you want me to tell you what happened. He's not even their father!"

"Listen," Thomas said. "Just so I'm clear on this whole... cat thing. Is it like this in other countries? What's it like somewhere else, in—France? I don't know, Asia?"

Billy narrowed his eyes. He shrugged, but he was frowning a little, with judgment.

"How should I know?" he said. "We may not be doing too good, but we're not unpatriotic. You sit here in my house... Come on, man."

Thomas stared at the wall for a long time. Billy had joined his wife in front of the TV, and now they were both laughing.

"Hey, listen!" Thomas said, standing up with resolution. "Billy?"

"Right here!" the man responded. "What's up?"

"I have to get going. Do you suppose there are still people I know—around?"

"Family? You got family?" came the voice, without the person.

"I had a wife. She left me, took my child with her. That's why I left town, more or less."

"Well, you go looking for them, ok?" said Billy. "Just don't make too many waves. Hey, tell me one thing, man. Was it worth it?"

"What, leaving them?"

"No. Coming back."

Thomas shook his head. He took three big steps to get to the door.

"Thanks a bunch for the liquor," he said. He closed the door behind him.

Outside, a few cats avoided him as he walked to the sidewalk. But they were looking at him with fixed eyes, paying attention. Thomas started running. He wasn't running toward a particular house, or street, or to find the way to another town. Cars passed him, and there were cats inside of them. Some cats sat on the roofs of houses. There were cats in trees, on lawns, cats crossing the street.

When he stopped running, he looked around as if there was nothing known in any direction, and there never would be again. A kitten came to meow at his feet. Thomas looked at it as if that was exactly what he was looking for. In a frenzied gesture, he grabbed it, walked with it to a canal. Grinning absurdly, he pulled open the rusty lid and, as he was preparing to drop the kitten, he saw four or five adult cats looking at him. They were coming toward him, with synchronized movements. He gave out a nervous laugh and lifted up the kitten with both hands, as if he had just pulled it out of the canal.

"The old kitten in the canal, how about it?" he said, pushing the kitten toward the cat that looked like the leader. He did not understand how, but he knew the cat was talking reassuringly to the kitten. He hurried to leave while they were still engaged in some sort of conversation.

Thomas walked away with casual gait, kicking stones with his foot. It certainly wasn't the welcome he'd expected, but in a strange way, it didn't seem all that bad. You wise up real fast when you have to. He breathed out his anger, breathed in the new day. He could not afford to be bitter. The scent of rebellion would be easy to trace, especially for something with a nose as refined as that of a cat.

Valley of the Horse

Heavy clouds bubbled over the city, the sun hovering behind them. Zak pushed the insides of his pockets with his fists, feeling coins and paper clips. He cursed the cold. Fall was morphing into winter, making him old. The same cats of every morning hid from view in the stink of garbage. The same tufts of grass sprouted among train tracks. Past the train tracks, there were a few dirty apartment buildings, then dry trees that bent around a crooked ravine. There, nobody had bothered to extend the city because, perhaps, it wasn't worth it. A crippled nature maintained a semblance of domain down the brown slope, among plastic bags and discarded tires.

This morning, something made him look twice in that direction— an intrigue he hadn't felt in years. Somewhere between the trees there was movement. A man under a tree—and something else. He stopped. He didn't want to be late to work, yet he could not turn around. He finally grasped the shape of a horse lying under a half-dried tree at the edge of the concrete.

The horse looked dead. The insinuation of disaster pulled him forward. He quickened his pace along the tracks, his shoes clumsy on the uneven ground. He threw a glance at the rust-ridden train car that had been on the tracks for as long he'd lived in the neighborhood. The iron breathed darkness.

He reached the ravine. The man and his horse looked like statues, except for the pained quivering of the animal's abdomen. In the interminable minute he spent trying to gesture, or to avert his eyes, he realized the man and his dying horse did not welcome him. He left.

He had never been good at witnessing pain. It had certainly backfired with April.

He made it to work and sank into the computer screen, shaking off the morning's unusual encounter. Yet he could not anticipate how obsessively he would go back to the tree in the space of a week, like an impotent king going back to see the oracle one more time, one more time.

The sun had not set when he left work. He seemed to be expecting something vital as his steps took him past the abandoned train car. They were still there by the tree, the horse trying to lift its head off the ground. The man was eating something from wrapping paper, bent as if to conceal his actual height. His thin, square jaw moved in a strange cadence, like a horse chewing grass.

The man looked up. He smiled, as if watching a fly make its way into a web. The horse saw the stranger and its eye bulged with whiteness. Pain hung in the heavy air.

"Easy, girl," said the owner, crouching to touch the dirty white neck. The horse released a troubled breath, laying its head on prickly grass.

Zak shivered: inside him, a brotherhood of bone and muscle felt the pain for a split second. He wanted to ask, "What's wrong with the horse," but, looking down into the slope at some broken shopping carts, he said:

"You live here?"

He could not yet grasp how misplaced this powerful, beautiful animal was, removed from the memory of wild air. It was waiting for death surrounded by geometry and cement. Beauty and death—did he not know that combination already? Before the word April could take shape, his thoughts sunk in haziness.

"You don't know me?" said the owner, looking askance. "You must have seen me around."

"Riding?" he asked, feeling foolish.

"You work near here, right?" the owner said. The horse whinnied and choked.

Zak stared at the animal, trying hard to bind with the world in front of him.

"What do you do—for a living?" he asked the owner.

"I'm a judge. Name is Ivy."

"Ivy. First name or last?"

The judge said nothing. The air thickened.

"I'm sorry, Judge Ivy." He meant, for the horse. "Well I'm—"

"I know who you are."

"I should get going," he said. "You think he'll live till morning?" His chin pointed at the horse.

"He's a she. I hope she makes it another day."

Zak nodded and turned away. The wind blew leaves up to his face. The horse blinked with the risen dust as she watched him walk away.

That night he dreamed that the horse was screaming like an engine or a train breaking its speed. In the morning, Laurie made him take an umbrella, and she did not ask why he left early. He had long suspected his wife preferred to spend her day alone. Not that she would ever leave the apartment—as if the TV and the computer mitght disappear while she was gone.

In the valley of plastic bags, the horse was still under the tree. Judge Ivy was not. It started to rain, so he opened the umbrella. As he approached, the horse struggled but could not stand up.

The rain pounded on the umbrella, so hard that it made him look down, at what was falling. Among water drops that dug pools in the dirt, there were things that moved when they hit the ground. Earthworms. They fell on his umbrella, on his shoes, on the horse. "Does this ever happen?" he wanted to say, and right then a voice near him said exactly that, "Does this ever happen?"

From behind the tree, or from the tree itself Judge Ivy stepped forward. He looked at the sky with gray, narrow eyes as he kneeled by his horse.

"I've heard of frogs," the judge said, "but never earthworms."

"Fish, too. But I thought it was a myth."

"Myth or no myth," said Ivy, "it can do nothing for my horse."

"A sign?" Zak averted his eyes from the agony on the ground. "Can worms be a sign?"

"Look," Ivy said, "read your fortune in worms if you want, but can you lower your voice? She's dying."

The worms stopped falling. The body of the animal was convulsing. She kicked the air with tremulous legs and stiffened for a few seconds as if wondering if it was a good time to end it. Then she relaxed and her breathing became even. The air carried the warm smell of horse. Perhaps it was indeed a sign—the horse, the worms, the judge. Some form of judgment day. Wouldn't April have wanted it that way? A single image of her surfaced: not a frail April, broken by anger, but a glorious April on horseback, many years before.

"Yeah, it's a sign." Ivy's voice was filled with spite. "The sky is spitting on us."

"It's the end of the—" Zak stopped, seeing the horse watching him. "Listen, you want the number of a vet I know?"

"Two vets have seen her already. I didn't want her put to sleep. I give her shots for pain. I wanted her to be on some real grass when she—"

"I'm sorry. I have to go," Zak said.

The earthworms looked like purple, twisted sticks. He stepped on a few, and the feeling stayed in his stomach for a while.

On the third morning, Zak did not go to the tree. There was no obligation. Yet guilt had been lodged in his chest for so many years that it took little for it to surface. When his coworkers sang happy birthday to a perky woman, his lips moved but he did not make sounds. Later, he retreated to the window.

Around noon, he saw a bird fall from the sky, wings flapping in the currents. No one in the office believed him. He made everyone gather, but he could not find the bird. In the end they retreated, leaving Zak like a prophet with no prophecies.

He went to the tree at the end of the day. Judge Ivy stood up when he saw him coming—not to greet him, but to block his way. His face was ugly.

"I'm sorry I didn't stop by this morning," Zak said.

Ivy did not speak. His prematurely wrinkled eyes were red and harsh—he had been crying. Zak took a step back, feeling irrevocably helpless, just as he'd felt that fated day at the hospital, in another life.

"Is she dead?" he whispered—an echo from the past.

The bones pushed the skin of the horse's back.

"No."

"Maybe it would be better—"

"Don't tell me what would be better. Matter of fact, I never asked you to come here."

Zak could do nothing but walk away. He could hear Ivy breathing angrily behind him.

That night, he had a dream of mountains with clouds on them, and he was walking on a dirt road. Clouds parted, as quickly as only dreams allow, and he waited for some great knowledge to shake him awake. The largest, most magnificent rock appeared before him, and he felt crushed by the mere sight. He fumbled to take his phone out, for a picture.

"Can't take pictures of that!"

He woke up. Laurie by his side looked like a dark, empty shell.

He did not go to the valley the fourth day. He could not understand why the judge, and that horse on the brink of death, were forcing him to watch himself—the bereaved and the accused—through the mirror of time. He craved a way back, a tunnel through the years to an innocence he wasn't sure he'd ever had.

On his way home after work, a girl joined him in the thickening evening. She couldn't have been older than twelve. She walked at his pace, pulling at her dirty old jacket. The girl sure was ugly. Her hair flew about, barely held down by a hat of some kind. She grinned. In one hand, she held a small tree branch.

He stopped.

"What are you doing?" he said.

She had a lot to say:

"I'm scared to go alone, and I have to go to school, and Mom isn't home yet. We're having Parent Day and my dad is coming but he said to meet him at the school, so I have to walk by myself between the buildings and it's getting dark. Can you walk with me to school? There's these boys who pick on me and they're waiting for me for sure. Please? My dad doesn't live with us and today he couldn't pick me up. But in three days he's getting me out of here," she announced proudly.

"Oh."

He had never thought there could be a school around there.

"It's that way," she pointed. "Do you work in this building? What do you do, sell stuff or what?"

"Maybe my soul." He laughed, knowing how awkward he sounded. "But you shouldn't trust strangers like me. I mean, not me personally but—"

She shrugged and took him by the hand, all the while holding on to her little branch.

"I've seen you other times. My mom's seen you. She says you're cute."

"Oh."

"My dad flies planes," she continued without a blink, and Zak looked up at the troubled sky. "He's taken me flying and he taught me to skydive. My dad knows a lot of people." She pulled him forward down a curving street among desolate yards and their junk.

He smiled. She was one of those kids who loved to make up stories. One day maybe she'd get caught lying in a big way, like he had. He tried to nod as she talked.

When they passed a huge, abandoned building, he cringed: this ugly liar could be setting him up. She could be the daughter of someone, walking him right into an ambush. He had nothing except a few credit cards and his keys. The girl kept talking, squeezing his hand. The building had no windows left intact, and the color of the brick had disappeared behind layers of black.

From the corner of his eye, he saw something darting behind the building, into the yard of a dilapidated house: it was a dark horse. The girl seemed to notice, and she pulled his sleeve and pointed:

"That's my father's house!"

He looked again, but where she was pointing he saw nothing but the house with no windows and with paint peeling off, shingles hanging.

"Christ." He frowned. "Where did you say your father was taking you in three days?"

The girl's attention had shifted. She showed him a small building surrounded by a wire fence, and said that was the school. He let go of her hand.

"Wait," she said, all serious. "Here, take this."

She handed him a crumpled drawing, from her pocket: a scrawny, deformed horse surrounded by crosses. He blinked. His throat was dry.

"You don't like to draw flowers and princesses?"

He watched her skip away.

On the fifth day, he left his apartment early, in a cold wind. He'd given Judge Ivy enough time to stop crying. He felt he knew him now, like an old friend.

As he crossed the tracks, he could tell that something was very wrong: the fallen horse was thrashing around noiselessly, with foam at its mouth. A wave of shame swept over him.

There were two men with the horse, and the one he didn't know was wearing rubber gloves dripping with blood.

"What on earth—" he started, as the horse settled into a deep sleep, dreaming of meadows. There was blood on the horse and on the leaves around.

"My friend is a surgeon," Ivy said. "He's given her a heavy sedative."

"A judge must have a ton of friends," said Zak. He laughed crookedly.

"I'm Pete," the man said, his voice unfriendly.

"So, Pete, what do a judge and a surgeon have in common?"

The three men looked at the sleeping horse.

"I suppose you both are fond of verdicts." He grinned.

"Right." Pete touched the sleeping neck of the horse.

The air was full of ambiguous waiting.

"So tell me, Judge Ivy, what do you judge?" Zak said.

"You mean *where*?" Ivy corrected.

"Never mind."

"Hey, we should go for a beer tonight," Pete said.

"No, tonight I have to be out of town," said Ivy. Say, would one of you mind checking on her early tomorrow? I know it's a Saturday."

"I can do that, sure," Zak said.

"Listen, Ivy." Pete's tone was soft now. "I feel bad for this horse. Tell me what else I can do."

Zak watched the two. There was such familiarity in their gestures that he wanted to drill inside their souls to find the exact source of their friendship, as if it offended him. Perhaps it was something strong like that he'd been looking for at the tree.

"At least she's not in pain now," Zak said.

"I gave her something stronger," said the surgeon. His face became remote. "I have horses, actually, up in the farmland. I know how it feels. Ivy, you should come ride there sometime. It'll do you good."

Zak's thoughts became cloudy.

"How can *you* know how it feels?" he said, surprised at his own anger. "If you have a hundred horses, do you know what it's like to be *this* horse, now? You've taken even feeling away from this animal! And you, Judge! Is suffering part of your expertise?"

"Who's this guy again?" Pete said to Ivy.

"Yes, exactly what I said," Zak shouted.

The other two looked at him without understanding.

"Did this horse ask you to pump her full of sedatives so you can watch her die?"

Oddly, he remembered having the exact same thought long ago, by April's hospital bed, with surgeons putting gloves on and taking them off. He had never found the answer to that old outrage. If only he could have undone her pain just as easily as he'd caused it.

No judge could give him what he had not been able to give himself.

"Not even the guy up there knows what pain is." He pointed at the sky. "I guess all you judges have that in common."

He turned and left.

The next day, he fought with his memories for a long time, and that went on even over lunch with Laurie. He did not want to go, but the thought that the mare was alone nagged at him until he gave in. With a mumbled explanation to his wife, he left her in front of the TV and walked out of the apartment.

The mare was awake. He looked around, suddenly timid. She was not in much pain—or else she had grown accustomed to her terrors. Rotting leaves made a thick bed for the dying mare. Her body was diminished. She had probably long forgotten how to be hungry. And yet he saw something there, a strength he could not understand. Powerless and forgotten, this horse seemed grateful for the breaths it could still take. She watched the comings and goings around her, weighing them, judging them in a way that people did not know how to judge. This horse, he thought.

There was recognition between them. She took his presence for what it was, and her eyes told him that she wanted to be in the world, alive. Overwhelmed with her shameless beauty, he reached down and touched the white face, feeling the obstinate bones to which life still clung. He caressed the long ear, hoping to transfer some warmth through it.

For reasons he could not possibly think of, he saw the mare pull her weight off the ground, struggling to lift her front legs. Her hoofs dug into the slippery leaves, nose pointing up, snorting and gulping the air. Dumbfounded, he stepped back, allowing her the dignity of her will to live. She was standing, looking at him with questioning eyes.

It was over as soon as it had started. Her legs remembered their weakness, and she kneeled down, without hurry. She let her body rest on her side again, still watching him.

Ivy was approaching.

"What did you do to her?" His voice was as rough as his words.

"You mean what *she* just did?"

"I saw you. Just be gone already!"

"But maybe she can still be—" he tried, but Ivy's eyes were nothing but hate. Zak retreated.

The seventh day was the last. He walked to the tree under a feeble morning sun. All he knew was he'd left something unresolved. There was a thing in him, an entity that he had to bring out of the dark. A dog ran from his path, growling.

The horse was there, and the two men. Everything was in place for his arrival, but something terrible was in the air. The men watched him with colorless eyes.

Then he knew what had driven him there that morning, and why everyone waited. Long ago, he had seen April draw her last breath. Now he recognized the mystery of life on the verge of leaving a body. A mute emptiness filled him.

And yet he did not expect the horse's legs to be missing.

"What have you done?" he whispered, staring at the small leaves that floated in puddles of blood.

Ivy's shapeless eyes were moist with tears. Pete looked at the ground.

"Don't worry," Ivy said. "She didn't feel a thing. Pete is good with that."

"You *made* him do that? And you?" He turned to the surgeon. "You listened to this lunatic? You're out of your minds." His words were empty and grating.

He knew it was coming, something from deep within. Suddenly, he saw himself from above, mutilated, with stumps where his legs had been. It was his own body he had come to watch, whose life was slowly dripping away. He knew why: it had been his body that had strayed from April, doomed her to unbearable pain, crushed her with the weight of the universe. Even now, he could not tell why he'd had more power over her in his betrayal than in his love, or why *someone's* body could have that power over another's *mind*. She'd called him filth and she'd wanted to chop his body to pieces.

He had not wanted to know exactly *what* April had taken, or if it had all been just an accident of pills and liquor.

He felt a sudden urge to dig a thousand rusty nails into his own arms and legs, to see his blood drip onto the crumpled leaves, to let his body drown in the pain he could never feel.

A small electric saw lay among the leaves. Judge Ivy was sobbing, caressing the fallen body.

"It's all because of you, Zak!" he shouted suddenly, lifting unrecognizable eyes at him. "Why couldn't you just leave us alone?"

Zak shivered. He could feel the miracle approaching. The morning grew still.

Grunting madly, Ivy bent with sudden resolve—his final, wild judgment. He lifted the body of the horse above his head and threw it into the valley below. Already dead, it rolled and rolled. It rolled away from the buildings, away from the men who did not understand. Just another useless, painful miracle of the city.

They stood there, looking at each other.

"How—" Pete started. His voice was lost in the valley below.

Punish the body to set the mind free. Yes, Zak thought, perhaps true freedom is the one privilege of those with nothing to lose. Somewhere in the distance, a horse had perished. Had her death granted him freedom from pain, and was that a fair trade?

The sky looked as if it wanted to snow, and the air smelled like snow. Zak took a step back, and finally lifted his eyes to look at Ivy.

"You, too, will be your own judge," Zak muttered.

For a long time—weeks, perhaps—he did not visit the place. It was Ivy who found him one day and asked him to walk together. There was something at the tree, he said, that he wanted to show him.

The ravine was still there, like a cavity, but at the bottom somebody had inexplicably built a white dome. Defiant, it stood against the brown grass of the snowless winter, among dirt and rocks and garbage. An old nun came out of the dome—an unassuming figure in black. The sting of what Zak had denied himself since April's death, even through years of married life, finally reached him. Looking down, he felt compelled to utter one question, although the answer stared at him silently from the valley of the dead horse, the same answer that pumped blood into his veins. He wanted to hear himself say it—it was as simple as that:

"Is it possible to live… without joy?"

The two men lingered awhile in silence. Below, the modest collector of souls busied herself by the dome in the cold, lonely morning. Their presence meant nothing to her. She was just eager to wash clean the bottom of the bottomless city.

Exorcism

Driving into the parking lot, she saw the man waiting, although he did not look at her car. Everything on his face was stricken and turned inward.

Only after she came out of the car did he register her presence. He watched her advance, nodding slightly to show her that yes, it was him. She held the paper lightly, as if afraid to touch it with more than her fingertips. He noticed it.

"Sorry I'm a little late," she said. They both looked at the ground. He cleared his voice to fill the silence.

"Antonio Reyes," he said boldly, to get it out of the way. His voice was gray, like his hair. "Mrs. Mitchell?"

She nodded, and her lips tightened as if to smile. She shook a hand that was dry as the dust, warm. A wrinkled labyrinth of lines had gathered the years on his palm, like the trunk of a tree.

"Thank you for coming," he said. "The girl, she sent you the message."

"Yes," she said, looking in his eyes, her eyes searching for what her voice could not ask.

"I don't know her," he apologized. "Tony—"

She nodded. His face twisted slightly, and his skin looked sun-beaten, innocently aged.

She did not give him the paper, and he looked at it in her hand again.

"I wanted to know—" he said, "if you could tell something was wrong— you know, in the summer."

She let out the breath she was holding in since she'd come out of her car. Her eyes watered.

"No, there was nothing. In fact, I always thought—"

"He's a good boy, very smart, right? He's my smartest one. You see, nobody in the family went to college before. My oldest son Javi, *su hermano*, doesn't have no patience. I taught him to work hard and he has a good job, but he never sticks to one thing. He didn't put himself through college. I don't know. What did I do wrong?"

"Tony of all people—I would never have guessed," she managed to say. She looked at him, wounds seeping from his whole body. His shoulders hunched as if waiting for a blow, standing there in the parking lot. The little *taqueria* did not have much business at that time.

Around them, the air was losing light, moving to evening.

"You wanted this," she said, holding out the paper. He did not take it but glanced at it as if she were holding a strange, sick animal.

"I had someone come to the house," he said, a sliver of shame entering his voice. "My sister told me, she said to do an exorcism. She brought somebody she knew."

She looked at him, eyes narrowing. Her hand retreated, half hiding the paper at her back.

"Why?" she said, and it came out as a whisper.

"It was... My son told me he was scared of something, like there was an ugly thing, *algo feo*, in him, that he never felt before," he said, wiping his cheek with a calloused hand. "He heard a voice tell him things in his head. I can't repeat them to you, you understand? When they did the exorcism, the whole family was there." He looked at the ground. "The voice didn't go away. He just didn't want to talk about it no more. I didn't know what to do. I went to church, I prayed. I was afraid. I told him, *hijo*, my son, go to church."

She opened her mouth to say something, but she just returned her eyes on him, waiting.

"My brother said to get him to a doctor, a head doctor. I don't know, what does the doctor know about it? His brother talked to him. He's close to his brother."

"He never saw a doctor?" she asked.

"We're God-fearing people, Mrs. Mitchell. The preacher talked to him, he told him to go to no parties no more. You understand how it is. You're— educated."

He covered his face with his hand, as if searching through his memories.

"How long had he been hearing voices?" she asked, and the small distance between them grew.

His hand withdrew from his face.

"A couple of months," he said. "That's it. He turned nineteen a while ago."

"He did?"

Blackbirds darted from a tree.

"I had no idea he was going through that," she said, trying to breathe out, let go. "He always had a smile on his face."

"Yes. He's a happy kid. You should've seen him growing up. Joking with his brothers all the time."

He paused, sticking his hands deep into his pockets, looking for something.

She looked away. The dusty Texas wind made her eyes water.

"In my class, he talked a lot," she said, her voice straining to comfort. "He was very quick to answer—and he loved stories. He always smiled."

"I wanted to show you his poems. I'll send them later, with the computer," he said, straightening his body.

"Poems?"

"He got really concerned with, you know, *los pobres*, poor people, he wrote it like a rap song or something. You'll see."

"He was one of the best students in that class," she said, her voice fading.

70

"He liked college. He signed up for the fall already."

She looked at him. His tears sparkled with pride.

"You wanted this, right?" she said and held the paper up for him. He took it quickly now, reading it right there, squinting, holding his chin in his hand as he stooped over the words. His son's words.

"What's it about? Is there anything bad in it?" he said, folding the paper in half, tucking it into his shirt. His sweat would soak it soon.

"It's about a love story, *Ethan Frome*." Then she was silent for a while, thinking, there were despairing words in that fictional story, words he may think she should have noticed. "It's a literary analysis, I didn't see anything strange in it."

"The night before," he said, "he went with his brother to a party. "He drank some, but not a lot."

She breathed in. It was coming, the thing she could not avoid was coming. She had given him the paper, and now she was ready to leave. She was nodding, looking at her car.

"They were up in San Antonio, and they were staying at a motel. They went back and his brother says he looked at Tony, and Tony... *mi Antonio*," he said trying to control his voice, "he was looking back at him with some eyes that he's never seen on his little brother before, like something dark was taking over him. His brother says he'll never stop seeing that look in his eyes."

She stood there, frozen.

"The next day—that's when he found him, on the motel bed. The gun was next to him."

She looked at his face again, and she knew the image that he hadn't even seen, that he had laid there in front of her for her to remember, was the one he would have in front of his eyes for the rest of his life.

"I just wanted you to know, because he liked your class," he said, when the silence had become too dark.

"I'll remember," she said.

His body shifted slightly away from her. He was letting her go now.

He watched her walk to the car, his hand on his chest, holding the paper. There were no voices left in that parking lot. The car drove away into a town where other fathers, other sons, went on.

At Taft Point

Bouncing from boulder to boulder and all around the Valley, shrill voices blend with the cries of high-flying birds.

By early November, Glacier Point Road had been closed for two weeks. At the trailhead for Taft Point and Sentinel Dome, the small parking lot was lined with California black oak, incense-cedars and tall white firs. Free of tourists after months of hikers sunup to sundown, the rounded spot where cars could park was white and silent now, in the rust-colored warmth of Indian summer. Massive, secretive forests surrounded the road.

Two white cars pulled into the parking lot. The doors did not open for a few seconds. Then, people started to emerge from both cars, taking in the sweet, robust air of Yosemite Valley. Two young, beautiful women with braided hair down to their waist and long, black skirts each brought a child. The blonde woman, lingering at the end of her teens, had a chubby toddler in her arms. The slightly older, red-haired woman waved to a boy of about six to get out. He dutifully circled the car to reach her, and she held him in front of her, close to her body, stroking his hair with vacant gestures as she waited for the driver to come out. The boy held a bird cage with a blue parakeet inside.

Three people came out of the other car. A middle-aged man with glasses carried a violin case. A young couple squeezed each other's hands, huddling together as if they were cold.

The last to emerge was the oldest man in the group—fifties or so—who had driven the car with the braided women in it. He was tall, hair parted in the middle in such an old-fashioned way that it could have started a new style. His dyed black hair showed a hint of gray roots, and he kept it long, like a Romantic poet might have. He narrowed his eyes toward the scattered fog among treetops. Even here, at the foot of the hike, the elevation was several thousand feet.

"Cara," he said to the blonde, and his voice startled a few bush creatures. "You tell me when you're tired of carrying the little one and I'll take over." The little one was the chubby toddler—a girl.

Cara nodded, closing her eyes. She didn't smile.

"Cheer up. Everyone, I want to see you smiling. This is one of the most beautiful places God gave us on this Earth. Who were you at the start of this very day? A mindless body in the shower. A crying child. Two mothers cloaked in the ignorance around them, to the point of being invisible. Two lovers crushed by these artificial pressures to become successful. A musician without dignified employment. Yet look how the embrace of the Valley is large enough, and forgiving enough for all of us."

He took off his leather jacket and threw it in the car.

"Won't you be cold?" asked the red-haired woman.

"Jennie, darling." He turned to her. "I do appreciate your care. A man cannot wish for a more dutiful companion. But we'll be walking uphill for some time. And there's a sun."

The boy held the bird cage up. The blue parakeet ruffled its feathers, turning its head to hear hidden birds.

"Not now, Huck. There's a time for everything," the man said. "We must go. Jennie, do you have water? For you and for Huck?"

The boy's mother said, "Yes," and pushed the boy gently ahead of her. She pulled her long, black skirt slightly, to give her feet some freedom of movement.

"The hike is about two hours," said the leader. He started walking ahead of the group. "What a shame," he said to no one. Everyone seemed to know what he meant.

They followed him, as he started on the trail to Taft Point. The young couple—he with a short beard, she with boyish, dark hair—walked behind everyone and for a while they held each other by the waist.

The other man, the one with the violin case, passed Cara and Jennie to walk by the side of the leader.

"Mister Rex," he said.

"Yes, Stan?" The tall, older man did not look at him as he took long steps on the wide trail.

They were in the heart of the woods, passing shedding oaks and green firs and pines.

"You could have insisted," said Stan. "The others—they just didn't have their minds made up yet."

"A shame, that's all there is to it," said Mister Rex. "I won't force anyone to walk with me. There's no signing of papers. The only true commitment is in the soul that has erased the chains of guilt and shame. Isn't that what all papers are for?"

He stopped, turned to look at the small group following behind. They all stopped, watching his face for a sign, a command.

He smiled. He opened his arms wide, lifting them toward the trees.

"Love is around us. Love is all that has true existence. Those who denied us have denied the only truth there is. They stayed behind to be with the herds and listen to lies. We have it all, right here."

He began walking again.

Cara, the younger mother, was still carrying her toddler in stern arms, while Jennie pulled Huck by the arm as the boy started to protest the fast pace. The bird cage dangled in his hand, the parakeet flying around in a panic.

"Jennie, tell the boy that the first stop is his," Mister Rex said.

Low, patchy clouds floated in the opposite direction. They unraveled gray arms toward the tops of the highest trees, to merge with the shimmering mist of late morning.

The first clearing came soon. The group gathered on a round rock to look at stretches of Yosemite Valley, the great shadows of granite towering over the sea of brown and green treetops.

"Now, Father? Mister Rex?" said the boy.

"God will witness now. Let it go."

The boy sat the bird cage on the rock. The young couple embraced, watching the little boy labor with the cage door.

"But it's going to be winter soon," the boy said.

"Do what Mister Rex told you," his mother whispered.

Mister Rex crossed his arms.

"You are mistaken, Son," he said. "Winter will never be coming. Let the bird fly for as long as God wills it to fly. Bear witness to freedom."

The boy opened the little door and put his hand in. The bird jumped on his finger, and this way he brought it out of the cage.

The blue parakeet hesitated. His beady eye looked up into the boy's face, to question the open air around. Then it flew. Mister Rex watched the boy, and the two mothers watched the father's eyes, trying to read something new in them.

The bird disappeared in a tree.

"I know you cry in your heart," the father said to the boy. "But for all of us, without a sacrifice, our souls are lost to the indifference of the world."

The group sang a song of praise, looking up and sending their voices forward into the mist. Huck sang the loudest.

On the trail again, the boy did not complain anymore. He walked fast, gloom on his face. The leader walked and hummed, now and then looking behind and smiling, showing his teeth. He looked pleased, the more he walked.

The young couple had become garrulous. They walked at a distance from everyone, pointing at nature, listening to the life hum in the crackling of gargantuan trees. They kissed often.

The mind's heaviness dissipated as the heart rose to spaces that birthed themselves ceaselessly all around. Gray monoliths looked weightless as invisible winds breathed from rock to rock to sky.

The younger mother passed the toddler to Mister Rex.

At the next clearing, they sat down in a circle. They drank water and ate apples. From the mossy rocks on which they sat, they could see across the Valley the granite giant called El Capitan—the centerpiece of the Sentinel Dome. Its bedrock anchored deep into the earth, the largest boulder looked like the forecastle of a gigantic ship, frozen in time.

Stan, the man in his forties, took out his violin. As the curves of the instrument touched his fine, long jaw, his dark eyes closed and he withdrew inward. Everyone's face was overtaken by longing, as the notes cascaded into the solemn distance. Soft at first, the bow caressed the strings, letting out inhuman waves of patterened sound that bounced around, merging with its echo. The bow slowed down to let the music linger, at home among the other earthly wonders. The pilgrims no longer had limbs, clothes, or names, but were part of something grand and eternal that breathed in tectonic rhythms. There was just a hint of mournfulness in the longer notes, but hope-filled trills quickly took their place. The clouds stood still.

At the end, Mister Rex got to his feet. He nodded at Stan, who stood up as well and with gentle hands he placed the violin at the base of a looming Douglas fir. In single file, the group found the path and started on their hike again. Stan turned his head to see the violin one more time, but now it was obscured by shrubs. He adjusted his glasses, or wiped something out of his eyes.

They were close to Taft Point, : where, not long ago, the summer months had brought hundreds of tourists in search of an easy, thrilling hike. The hump of rock became visible and towered above the tallest trees. The last part of the hike would be steep, to the greatest view of all.

"This stop," the leader said, slowing down, "is for Chase and Melinda."

The young couple glanced at each other and halted. The two mothers looked at the ground, holding their children a little closer.

"Do not shield the children's eyes. This is the greatest gift of love that this rock will ever know."

"But… Mister Rex," said Chase, holding Melinda's hand.

"Do you love her?"

"Of course I do."

"This is the time to show it from the core of your being. Nature, God's grand stage, will bear witness to the essence of love, stripped of all social pretenses."

"Can we hide behind those bushes?" said Melinda, her voice choked with anticipation.

"Do you hide your soul from God?"

Melinda smiled and blushed just a little. She started to take off her jeans. Young, deer-like legs. She took off her sweatshirt. Her bra. Compact, silky breasts. The six-year old tried to look away, but his mother gently turned him back around, to watch. Stripped of his clothes, Chase was hairy.

Everyone sat down as Chase and Melinda moved a bit farther, on a patch of grass. Their bodies fell to the ground, awkward at first, then forgetting the others. The trees crackled and buzzards cried high above, innocuous end rhymes to the poetry of breath. The two newly released—and suddenly relieved—human animals tumbled, grass sticking to their perspiring skin. Melinda's careless pitch set a few birds flying. The toddler was squirming in her mother's grip. The leader put his arms around the two young mothers, drawing them close to him as they all watched. The contortions ended in slow motion, and the trembling ceased. The lovers remained embraced for a while, eyes closed, their young bodies still tangled. Melinda sobbed with quiet joy, rubbing her cheek against Chase's bearded face.

Minutes later, the group was on the move again. It didn't take long to reach the rocky cliff, the awe-gilded boulder overlooking the Valley. Bridalveil Fall rumbled soundlessly in the distance—a thin strip of water. El Capitan was in full view, majestic like the migration of continents, standing guard above the coniferous Valley.

But the group didn't lie on their stomachs to peek below, like tourists. They did not need to be that close to the edge to see how far the rest of the earth was.

All eyes turned to the leader.

His voice was strong, stony. It fell and rose in declamations that mimicked the peaks lining the horizon. Transfixing, like the landscape.

"My blessed children," he said. "Let me start by saying I love you all very much. I declare it to these mountains. Here, history witnessed the running of Indians from their lands."

The others made a small circle around their leader, nodding as their furtive eyes were drawn toward the wide Valley below.

"All over this country, the Natives were enslaved, ridden like horses when Columbus' men were too lazy to walk. They were taken to Europe and died by the thousands. Their arms were cut off. They worked in mines. Husbands and wives saw each other as seldom as every ten months—and they were too tired to make love. Among the Tainos and the Arawak people, there were mass suicides. People poisoned their babies with cassava."

"The Lord received them in His arms," Cara murmured.

"The Lord will not accept one man to be the servant of another," the leader said. The shadows on his gaunt face deepened. "When the government puts chains on you, your love is stunted. Your only freedom, then, is the Kingdom of Heaven."

They joined hands, looking up to receive the knowing gaze of the leader.

"They will tell you that nature is indifferent," he continued. "Look around you. Nature is love. This is not an indifferent nature, but the guardian of our life-force. If you go back there, you will find only indifference. Consumerism will lull your soul. What do you become? A void of emotion, a non-spirit. *That* is the ultimate indifference. Need I say it? *That* is the opposite of love."

He was silent for a while. The mountains awaited the offering.

"It is time."

Mister Rex nodded toward Chase and Melinda, still shivering in each other's arms.

"Don't look down," he said. "Look to the sky, where your heart belongs."

The young couple stood at the edge of the rock, smiling through tears. They took each other's hand. "One, two, three," Chase whispered, and their legs pushed against the rim. They were gone.

The leader nodded toward the violinist. The man took his glasses off, dropping them to the ground. He walked to the edge.

"Love is light," he said, and entrusted his body to the Valley.

The leader looked at his two lovers. He moved to Cara, and he kissed the forehead of the little girl in her arms. He kissed Cara, briefly, on the mouth, and squeezed her elbow. He stepped back.

Cara moved to the edge and turned her back to the void. She looked in the eyes of her man, her life. She tightened her arms around the girl and she took in a long breath, as if to last her on her way down. She disappeared.

It was then that Huck, the boy, pulled his hand from his mother's grip and ran away from them. His mother screamed.

"Stop him! Stop him, Rex!"

Looking at her, his eyes darkened. He ran after the boy. "Huck! Huck!" he called.

He brought the boy in his arms, patting his red hair. He stood in front of Jennie.

"You first," he said to her. "Say goodbye to your son."

Jennie smiled, her mouth trembling. When she kissed the boy's cheek, Huck screamed and kicked against his father's stomach.

"It's all right," she said, repressing a sob. "We'll all see each other very soon."

She looked at Mister Rex, and lifted a hand to caress his stern, bony face one more time.

"I can't take this…" she murmured and turned in one abrupt move, running full-speed toward the precipice. She left the world without a sound, as her son screamed in the arms of the leader.

"Are you going to be a man about it?" Mister Rex asked, turning the boy's face toward his face. "I love nothing else as I love you right now, do you know that?"

The boy looked at him. Something in his father's eyes commanded him to be quiet. The man's eyes were gray, like granite. Mountains flickered in the depths of his dark pupils.

"I love you, daddy," the boy whispered.

The man bent his head to kiss the top of the boy's head. It was an honest kiss—the opposite of indifference. He sat the boy down on the rock.

"Give me your hand," he said.

The boy obeyed. Together, they stepped closer to the edge. As the boy's eyes met the void, he took a step back. His father tightened his grip.

"Now!" The man said.

"No—" The voice broke.

The larger figure tumbled in space, pulling after him the smaller, screaming figure.

The air was filled with bird cries. It didn't take long for the scream to blend with the enormity of the sky, floating downward like a bird returning home, to some eternal, long awaited nest.

Away from the Flock

"It doesn't hurt."

The two boys hit Andrew's legs again.

"Did it hurt now?"

Andrew shook his head, his eyes moving from one to the other. They were all about seven or eight.

"How about this?" One of the boys scratched Andrew's face.

"It doesn't hurt."

"You're lying."

"It's my turn," Andrew said. "I'm gonna kick both of you and you aren't allowed to cry."

The two boys looked at each other. One of them turned and ran away from the low bushes, to the water. Now he was in full view of several other children, and one of the adults.

"Come back here," Andrew shouted.

The boy started running by the water, along the tree line. The geese ran away from his path.

"And you? Are you going to run too?"

Andrew was watching the boy, eyes wide like a stalking cat's. He put his tongue between his teeth.

"If you hit me," said the other boy, "I'll tell Father Achon I found you with your pants down."

"So tell him."

"And you were grabbing yourself."

"So what?"

Without warning, Andrew launched at the other boy and hit him between his legs. The boy's surprised grunt escaped along with the air in his lungs, and he folded himself in two, on the ground.

Andrew stepped away from him. A vague, distant clamor reached him as he looked at the scattered children throwing stones in the pond, or running. One tall figure in black stood watching him from the other side, and his robes fluttered in the wind.

Goose Neck Ridge Retreat was right on top of the hill, its main building hidden between red maple trees and oaks. With the boys gone to the pond, it was still and quiet when the middle-aged woman with wheat-color hair came to stand in front of it. She could have gone unnoticed, small as she was, had she not been the only woman entering the building in many hours.

In the large hall, she examined the oversized Jesus in the style of naive paintings that stretched across the entire back wall. A flock of geese was flying above his enormous head, and in the corner of the painting, a fox held a goose by the neck.

"You have a boy at the retreat?" a man's voice said.

She turned, startled by the bald man next to her.

"I'm looking for Father Achon," she said. Her voice was as diminutive as her small frame.

"He's at the lake, with the boys. Five minute walk that way," he said. "You can't miss it."

She turned around and left the building. As she went down the steps, she seemed to remember she was in a hurry. Her face hardened. On the path through the woods, she was running.

At the pond, geese quacked out of her way as she came into the clearing. The grass was groomed. Benches and trees aligned along the water's edge. Children, and two men in black robes congregated near the benches.

Her son, Andrew, ran toward her when she was close enough to be recognizable. He stopped midway, looking behind him as if asking for approval from the two men. He waited for her and took her hand, and they walked together to the group. She stopped and sent the boy back with the children, saying simply, "Wait for me there." He joined the others, but kept his eyes on his mother.

She was looking at the older man, Father Achon. He lifted his head as if to smell the air. She took a few more steps and stood in front of him, all the children watching. His hand patted the round head of a child.

"*Miss* Garrett," he stated. He lifted his hand to quiet the boys.

She didn't say anything for a while, but did not look away.

"You came to see Andrew?" he said with slight impatience.

"Can I talk to you?"

Her voice was brisk.

"Of course." His face expanded in a generous smile. "I'm here."

"No. I mean, can we walk together," she said. She looked at the pond, taking a deep breath.

"God's path is open to those who choose to take it." He smiled at the boys, then turned to the very young man next to him. "Brother Michael, stay with the children. Will you tell them the weeds story, please," he added, his voice secretive. "Parable 12," he said louder.

He stepped toward the woman. He was tall, strong. She did not look up but started walking, as his hand reached toward her back, to guide her. He had to quicken his pace to keep up, as she started on the small trail around the pond. They would be in plain view of the group the whole time.

"Jesus said, whoever loves father and mother more than me is not worthy of me," he explained, keeping his voice calm and kind as if talking to a child.

"We do not encourage parents—"

"How is Andrew?" she said over his voice.

"—to join us at the retreat."

"Yes. How is Andrew?"

He looked at her. His eyes narrowed:

"He is well. He prays, he reflects. He is good in the game room."

She looked at the group they were leaving behind. Benches and trees were filling the distance between them and the flock of children. Her face turned sad.

"Andrew likes games," she said. "That's why I wanted him to go. He spends hours—"

"Yes, you did right by him," Father Achon nodded.

She looked at him, walking a few feet to his right.

"But you let them play."

"We have games to strengthen their bodies, and games to open their minds," he said. His chest buoyed him to look even taller. "We have team games. The children learn to be humble. You see, Miss Garrett, even St. Augustine didn't think he could live the Beatitudes. Then he saw simple people, humble people live in self-denial." He looked down. "That's when he knew he could do it."

She bent her head too, frowning.

"Father Achon."

"What is it, Miss Garrett, what are you worried about? Worries make us weak in the face of our challenges. Andrew—"

"I know."

"*Faith.*" He looked at the sky. "Do you pray, Miss Garrett? You must know, prayer is not just sitting on your knees in the pew. I see you there every Sunday. Prayer is a way of life."

"I know." She looked at the grass, avoiding goose droppings.

"Prayer is what we think about through the day. The strongest faith is not—"

"Are you molesting my son?" she said, placing her body right in front of him, blocking his way.

"Am I what?"

"Molesting," she hissed. "You are molesting my boy," she shouted now, her face contorted and ugly.

He stopped in his tracks and looked at the group across the pond, as if they could hear. It seemed as if he were no longer breathing, only listening. Facing him, the mother made no other noise. The trimmed bushes quieted their rustling. He blinked a few times, still looking in the direction of the children.

"Miss Garrett—" He staggered slightly, as if recovering from a dizzy spell. "Please, never say that again."

She scrutinized the group across the pond, like a bear watching her cub. There, all the children had lifted their arms, looking at the sky. Father Michael's arms swayed like tree branches in front of them.

"You did not answer the question," she said. Her voice came out soft and forlorn.

He looked straight at her:

"No. I absolutely do not."

She seemed to absorb his most minute expressions.

"Father Achon. I've been coming to your church for fifteen years."

"Yes, I know. You are—"

"You know I'm raising a child on my own. You've heard all my confessions."

Sweat had gathered on his forehead, where vertical lines converged in a frown.

"Miss Garrett, we all owe each other love, whatever our flaws are. Love is our debt to each other. We owe taxes to the state, we pay taxes. We owe honor to our soldiers, we honor them. But we owe love to everyone."

Her head bent as if under a blow, yet her chin was hard.

"You dare speak of love!" she said. "Do not—" She swallowed, trembling.

He stepped closer.

"I *will* love everyone," he said, "even those who are evil enough to say such things about me. I will not slight even the lowliest in paying my debt of love. But you have to tell me who said such a thing. And when."

"Father Achon, why would I believe you?"

The geese were silent.

"Believe."

"I cannot leave my son here, you understand." She looked again at the group of children. "Not until I know for sure."

"You don't believe me? Is my word worth nothing to you, Miss Garrett?" His voice grew strong. "How long have we known each other?"

"Andrew has become withdrawn. He plays all day, those video games," she said fast, as if to herself. "He is hateful when he plays the shoot'm'up games, and I can't stop him. He has nightmares. I can't explain how he's changing. I thought the retreat would help him."

"Boys copy each other, Miss Garrett, you know that. They're young. Young in spirit, young in faith."

"They are so young!" she said with sudden force.

"Do you know the parable of the ten virgins?" He smiled at her from his towering heights. "Just as those wise virgins, the boys will take with them the oil of faith, and they will take more than they need, to last them in their daily life."

"Oil!" she grimaced.

He looked at her, dumbfounded.

"Yes."

"Fucking *oil*!"

Her voice broke into a cry. He took her by the shoulder, but she stepped away.

"Miss Garret. I never claimed to understand the ways of God completely," he said, composing himself again as he talked over her head, into the woods beyond. "An arrogant theologian would say God speaks to him every day. I am not arrogant. I will search for answers until the day I die." He talked fast, retrieving all the words he could from the pages he sermonized. "Jesus, you see, did not want to bring the Pharisees into his group of disciples. And why? Because they could no longer learn, they had closed minds. He wanted the sinners to join him, because they had much to learn. He could change them. He could teach them to love."

"A child is not a sinner!" Her teeth clenched to the point that it looked like it hurt. "You can't call a child a sinner!"

"We are all sinners, Miss Garrett. Will you pray with me for our imperfections? Ezekiel 34:16," he said, his blue eyes consumed with something from within. "I will seek the lost, I will bring back the strayed. I will bind up the injured, and I will strengthen the weak." His voice grew incantatory.

"Enough!" she shouted. "Enough! You may not think much of me, but I am a *mother*. Mothers don't stop."

A flash of her teeth sparkled for a second, and her breathing turned into a growl. Then she turned abruptly. She sprung away and left him there, anchored solidly in the ground, rooted and unbent.

He waited for her to be far away, and he let a scornful smile illumine his face, his eyes lifting to the tree-colored sun. Just for a moment. From a distance, he watched as the woman grabbed her son's hand and pulled him away from the flock. Shaking his head, he followed with storm-blue eyes the woman prodding her sullen child, until they disappeared on the trail back to the Retreat Center. With measured steps, he made his way back.

Drifters

Bird cries splintered in his ear like shards. The forest danced with flickering ghosts. He wondered if water would silence his guilt. He plunged. His body broke the murky surface. The water covered him like a uniform and the sunlight disappeared. He tasted the thick swamp. An image of marching soldiers floated before him. Forlorn soldiers in the frozen swamps of Europe, like beaten dogs. He couldn't remember when that image had gotten plastered to his brain. His lids struggled in water the thickness of blood, and he reached with his hands to part the grasses on the bottom. Whether the nebulous fish led him to that spot, or his soldier-like instincts, he was now facing a body rolling among the bales of algae.

In seconds that lasted hours, he was pumping the boy's chest, and the boy was coughing up water. Martha reached them just then, and he let her rush at her child like a tigress.

Online, Kevin had mentioned the war once, in passing. He just thought he'd add a little suffering to his persona—a harmless shortcut. That was the plan. But then her messages started to make him smile. Before they even met, she was already confessing: her failures, her parents' failures, the jobs she couldn't keep, the lovers. The flashes of anger and guilt were like wild flowers she was throwing at him. He asked about her boy and, to make himself benign, he evoked his nephews and nieces.

They met. He became instantly addicted to her sympathy when she looked at him, the way she tried to see the world through his eyes. The way she would blow the smoke away from him, watching him all the while. The way she was afraid to touch him at first, because she said loving him would burden him, would intrude upon his memories.

He said to her things like, "I carried a wounded girl once, and her legs looked melted."

She would answer in the strangest way, not avoiding the image, but pushing herself upon it, trying to displace it. She would say, "Pick me up as if I'm wounded, as if my legs are gone."

She was light as a child in his arms, and she'd feel his shoulders, muscular, and right then she would kiss him. She asked for a measure of his pain every day, extracting it against his will.

The only time when he agreed to tell her a full story was when she asked if he'd lost anybody very close. At first he only said, "Martha, what do you think?"

"I don't think. I know you did." Her frail, tobacco-stained fingers covered her eyes. "When I lost my mother, she was in a dark room for months," she said. She let her hand fall, releasing the memory. "I cleaned her sheets and I carried her bedpan. I hurt so much for her that I started hating her, because I had to spend my nights worrying, remembering her voice when she was healthy, wanting her to talk like that again. I was sixteen and I could not stand her gurgling voice, and her groggy eyes when she tried to make me stay in the room so she could look at me. I had that chance, to sit with her for days, but I always left her room in a hurry and I went to cry in my room instead of talking to her. It must have been very different for you. One night you were playing cards with a buddy, the next morning he was in a body bag. I don't know that hurt. It must be something you still think didn't really happen—part of you does."

"Why do you want to know that hurt?" he asked. "Yes, I'm sure you're not afraid that when you watch a movie with your best friend Bessie, it could be the last time you see her alive. You don't have to wish that 'Get lost' wasn't the last thing you ever said to her."

"That's why I asked, Kevin. Who was the closest friend you lost? I want to remember him with you. Please." Her cloudy, half-closed eyes were filled with hunger for that something she wanted him to give.

"Grief isn't something you share. You want to hear it, but how can that possibly help me?" he asked.

"Kevin. You grieved for three years," she said. "Now you're with me. If you trust me at all, come back to the real world."

"You're not my therapist."

He let her carry that thought around for the two days he didn't see her, while he tried to find enough reasons to disappear. He'd allowed this to go on long enough. Yet all he could think about was that viper-like body slithering under a small dress, and he craved the bite. He'd give her the story she wanted. In the end, he patched together the bits and pieces he found online, on the usual blogs he browsed for hours. Five people became one: Garcia, who lost his buddy Mark Logan to a roadside bomb and went on a killing rampage. Two other friends who were killed drinking their coffee together. "The Punk" carried to safety two soldiers at once. He added some details as he looked at blurry war pictures on the blogs. He felt proud of the final product, as if it justified at long last his own inadequacies.

He put on a broken face and went to see her, ready to tell.

Her hand was on his shoulder.

"His name was Derek," he said to her.

She drew breath quickly, avidly. She took his face in her hands and he looked above her, at some suspended flow of collective memory.

"If you tell me about him, maybe everything will become real again. Maybe you won't sleepwalk anymore."

She was beautiful when she said that, and he wanted to touch her light hair. Then his eyes moved past her again, to the story she was hungry to hear.

"Derek was a Staff Sergeant," he said. "He became like an older brother to me. We shared all our care packages, and we read our letters to each other. He always made an extra coffee for me. We bullshitted over that coffee every morning. It was like our own ritual. We were in the same Infantry Regiment. Once we were going from Baghdad to Fallujah, and we knew it was one of the worst missions out there. I didn't even see how the attack started—I saw this smoke coming from our camp. I didn't have time to think about it but I could tell many must have died there. I learned later that he'd died of a gunshot wound to the head. Man, that really changed me. I wanted revenge. But when we ended up blasting this woman with a Mark 19 grenade launcher one time, and she turned out to be carrying a grocery bag, I couldn't see that as revenge. Nothing, no one I ever shot is going to fill the gap. Revenge is bullshit."

She listened to him go on about how he hated, and how he was sorry for those people he killed. She forgot to draw from the cigarette, her hand shaking. She was always shaky—she said she had an overactive thyroid.

"In a way, this is how we felt here at home," she said. "Sometimes sorry, sometimes hateful. But for us, those feelings came from a blank space, you know what I mean? We couldn't know what was really going on there, so we imagined. Our feelings were abstract, so sometimes they got stronger that way. Phantasmagoric."

"I know."

"I need *real* feelings," she said before she took him to her bedroom.

In a few days, she became more concerned about what he was going to do with himself. She asked him, "Would you feel less of a man if I helped you find a job?"

He looked at her and tried to smile.

"What question is that? Of course I want a job."

"I wish you could become a cop. I always thought cops were sexy."

"Cops?"

"At least their uniforms," she laughed. "I like their uniforms."

He frowned.

"Iraqi kids said the same thing," he told her. "They said they liked American uniforms. When I saw their bodies blown up, liking our uniforms wasn't cute anymore."

Her wide eyes made him avert his.

"You didn't have to say that to me."

Martha did try to help him find a job, but it was hard. At Denny's, where she worked, they were sacking people at the time, so it couldn't have worked. She asked friends, and got a few phone numbers that didn't pan out.

He said his parents couldn't support him now, and he couldn't even stand the sight of them, because he knew they judged him. They did not believe in PTSD, he said, and he didn't even drink as much as some of his war buddies. They wanted him with a job, out of the house. He didn't want her to meet them.

"Fuck your parents," she said to him. "You came back, and this is what they do? They can't even appreciate you? If my last boyfriend was half the man you are, I wouldn't have kicked him out. In fact, he kicked himself out. Same thing with my kid's father. Just wasn't a real man. He couldn't even stop his friends from groping me in the bars. Now I'm supposed to make a man out of this boy by myself?"

She cried then. She said that if he let her love him like he deserved to be loved, he could move in with her. But she said if he planned to run away later, to please tell her so she'd stop caring before it was too late.

He moved in. That was when Ted, the boy, finally met him. She'd never brought Kevin home when the boy was there. She had first wanted to see that he wasn't one of those guys who ended up getting dragged away by the police, drooling and coked out.

"I only drink beer," he had said.

He didn't bring much except some clothes with their hangers, and a grimy shaving kit. She bought a few things for him—they went to Walmart together.

"We'll get through all of it," she said. "It makes me so angry you can't get a therapist without insurance. I swear I'll go to community college to be a psychiatric nurse. I'm too old for medical school, but that way I'll treat both of us. Waitress is not a goddamn career."

The boy, Ted, was reluctant at first. He said to Kevin, "You're worse than my dad." From an eight-year-old, that hurt a little. In their bedroom, Martha explained what the kid had meant: when he wasn't at some bar, his dad would just sit around the house and watch TV. He would spit on the floor and yell at the kid to bring him beer.

Kevin asked Ted to watch TV with him, and the boy didn't want to. He'd just stand in the door and stare. Then the boy cursed and kicked when Martha tried to take him to his room, and she cried. Kevin took Ted to his room and closed the door. To talk to him, man to man.

"My mom thinks you're some war hero, but my mom is fucking stupid," Ted told him.

The skin on his face was strangely dusty and sharp, as if he was thirty, not eight.

"What is with the war thing?" said Kevin. "Your mom is not stupid, and I don't want to hear those words from you again. We gotta learn to get along, Ted. How's this: you'll be *my* hero if you're nice to your mom."

"Nobody likes her. She's a bitch," the boy said.

"You don't like your mom either?"

The boy was quiet.

"Do you know how lucky you are to have her?" Kevin said.

"Lucky my ass," said the boy, and Kevin raised a hand as if to slap him. "I'm not afraid of you. My mom's boyfriends beat her, you're not so tough. What makes you so tough?"

"Ted, I promised your mom you and I can be friends. I will never hit your mom—or you. That's what a tough guy does, buddy. He only hits a man who jumps at him, you understand?"

"What makes you a hero?" the boy said. "I think you're full of shit."

Kevin stared.

"Ok. I saved a couple of my buddies once, Ted. That's one thing your mom is talking about."

"Like how? Tell me."

"You too with the stories? Come on."

He had no choice. He told the boy that one time a car blew up in front of him on a bridge and he had to dive into a river. It was a very dirty river because that was the only kind of river in Iraq. He saved two wounded soldiers, and another two were already dead. He didn't want a medal.

He heard Martha crying behind the door, and he came out and asked her why. She said it wasn't sadness. She started laughing while she cried.

"I can't remember the last time a man sat down with Ted to tell him a story," she said.

Two more days passed and Kevin and the boy were shouting at the TV together, at the football players, hurling popcorn through the air. The boy brought out his football and asked Kevin to play.

"Only if you stop comparing me to your dad, or your mom's other boyfriends," Kevin said.

It was about three months after he'd moved in with them that Kevin started sleepwalking. He said he used to do that in his parents' house, and now it had come back. He would sit up in bed and he would shiver, covering his ears. If she tried to talk to him, or if she started crying, he'd run into the street, shouting, "Don't touch me!"

He told her it was like he was carrying the dead with him, and he felt it was contagious. Making love to her became a fully clothed business, but she swore to him that nothing he did to her would drive her away.

What he didn't tell her was that he felt as if a nail had been lodged into his temple, all the time. A feeling in his throat as if the lies had been crammed in there for too long. He almost told her, but he stopped.

Then he almost told her in their one fight that convinced him he had to leave. They were outside together, raking the first fallen leaves.

"You won't touch me because of my scars?" she asked that day. They were in the kitchen, eating cereal. "Those are old scars, I promise."

"No," he said. "It's not about you cutting yourself. That's not as weird as you think. It's just that—it's hard for me to let my body be exposed. Or to see you expose yours."

"You didn't feel like this at first. I thought it was all falling into place."

"I know. But things come back."

"You have to let it all out," she said. "You've brought too many demons with you, and they're standing in the way. Tell me, what were you most afraid of back there, in Iraq?"

"You're crazy."

"But that's what you said you loved about me."

"No—I mean, you're fucked up, Martha."

"I know a woman whose husband is also a vet. One day he snapped and he put seventeen bullets into the wall, in their house. Don't you think her fear was real?"

"Am I competing here?" he said.

"No, Kevin. The point is that she is still with him, and that's because she loves him. I just want you to trust me again."

"You want me to shoot at your house or what?"

"You don't need to get aggressive."

"You know what, smoking makes you neurotic. You should quit."

"You sound just like my exes. Does it make you feel manly if you call a woman neurotic?"

"*Manly*? What is this all about?"

"I'm not your enemy. I wasn't in the war with you."

He threw the rake against the tree.

"Will you stop it with the war?"

"You want to beat me, don't you? Come on, hit me, maybe that will make you feel better."

He grabbed her by her elbow.

"Kevin, why can't I help you?" Her face twisted so she wouldn't cry.

"God, I don't *want* you to help me." He let go of her elbow. "Why do you love me anyway? Can't you see what garbage I am? Human garbage. Don't you see what you've brought into your house?"

"You can't make me not love you," she said.

"How much do you bet I can? Stop sucking other people's pain and start dealing with your own pain, why don't you? You can't save me. You can't love the *real* me."

"If you think pain is the only thing we have in common, you're so wrong," she answered. "When are you ever going to be happy? Are you doing any favors to the dead if you turn away from life?"

"What do you know about the dead? I don't even know anything about them. This has gone too far. This simply has gone too far," he said, his voice filled with disgust.

He stayed angry at her for two days. She stopped mentioning the war, but he noticed new scars on her arm, when her sleeve was up. Her shaking got worse.

One day, he heard the boy tell his schoolmates about the dirty river where Kevin had saved the wounded friends. Ted had an actual crowd listening as the school bus stopped, and even the driver gave him a minute to finish the story. The boy's grin was big as he told his own version of the story. "Gun shots from everywhere." "Car flipped three times in the air." "River was filled with blood." "They gave him a medal." He pointed at Kevin taking out the garbage. Faces of children turned to look from bus windows, and Kevin frowned and went quickly into the house.

He finally brought himself to tell Martha he was moving out. He would not say why. First, she screamed, kneeling on the kitchen floor. She locked herself in the bedroom for hours, and he took Ted outside to play catch. He told him his mother had a toothache.

When she came out, she was calm. She asked him for one more chance. She wanted a family outing, a picnic and a hike in the woods. There was a place with a lake, and she said that was the best therapy, and why hadn't they done that before. He said yes because Ted was there. Then the boy got on top of a chair and jumped on it, shouting "Pic-nic! Pic-nic!" until Kevin took him down.

They took cold cuts and grapes in plastic bags. The neighbor gave them their chocolate lab, Spock, to take with them, because the dog liked to run around and never got a real chance. The boy had taken care of the dog before, so he hugged the dog all the way to the lake. His mother had never let Ted get a dog.

Kevin was sitting with his back against a tree, telling Martha she was too good for him. She was crying silently. That was when he saw the dog jump into the lake, from the corner of his eye. That would have been a trivial observation had it not been for the boy's cry:

"Mom, Spock is drowning! I'll save him, like Kevin did!"

The boy made a big splash, with his clothes on, and Kevin knew that the boy did not swim.

Martha's piercing cry happened at the same time as Kevin jumped to his feet. They both watched for only a second how the boy came up—a fluttering shoulder and a head, a swollen jacket twisting with splashes, sinking again. The dog was already back on shore.

They both ran. With every step Kevin took toward the lake, one thought punctuated his foot hitting the ground: she would not, she could not, she must not forgive him. If the boy died, he had to tell her to kill him too. How had she not seen that whole time that he was just a crook and a loser, who hadn't returned from Iraq but from a stint in jail?

He had never really sleepwalked, either.

As Martha embraced her child, crying, Kevin kneeled next to them and reached to touch her shoulder.

"Martha. You have to stop believing all my lies."

Both Ted and Martha looked at him, the boy still coughing out mud.

"If this is going to work, you have to stop asking me to lie. It's all lies, Martha, all of it."

Martha stood up. She looked down at him, and down at her child.

"I know," she said. "I know."

Rabbit in the Hat

"He looks like a fish," Mrs. Martin said with a wide-mouthed laugh. Her dress glittered as it shook around her bones.

Her husband nodded while his small shoulders did the laughing. He motioned with his hand for her to lower her voice. In their small group, everyone held a glass of wine. Mrs. Martin bent over the table to pick up a deviled egg.

"Your wife doesn't seem too fond of Morris," the tallest man in the group said. "Don't you and Morris go way back at the museum?"

"Maybe—I think I could be his oldest coworker. I don't remember. But, you see, my wife has good taste in men."

"Still, you're friends, I assume?"

"Well, you do become close after so many years," Mr. Martin said. "It's been forty years for him, right? I still have a few left in me."

"Honey, yes he is your friend. You're the one who's never been mean to him, right?" said his wife.

"Never," he answered. "But he makes himself an easy target."

"What do you mean?" the corpulent wife of the tall man asked.

Mr. Martin scanned the people around the large room. Small groups just like theirs filled the space with discordant choirs of polite talk. As the wine refilled more and more glasses, the room became less restrained, the murmurs turning into impertinent bursts of unguarded conversation.

Around the escargot and bruschetta table, a group of artists and art promoters had become the loudest.

"But where on earth is Morris!" exclaimed a voluptuous woman pushing middle-age. "His own retirement reception, his own house, and he's letting us wait?"

"Margie, you know Morris," said a younger man, touching her elbow. "He keeps people guessing."

"Yes, Pete, you would know! You always tease him about his size, and he never dignifies you with an answer."

"He's just so… *petit*! I don't blame women for staying away from him."

Margie gave out a sharp laugh. She gulped down the rest of her wine and three men reached for the bottle to fill her glass.

"Morris is sweet, I guess," she said. "Who else would offer his own house for his retirement party? We were the ones supposed to surprise him with a restaurant party, right?"

"His house is impressive," said Tim Wyatt, the museum's art liaison. "Just look at the statues in the corners of the room."

"Margie," said a small, balding man, folding his arms to his chest. "Morris isn't exactly everyone's father figure at the museum. But I give him this: he's never held any grudges."

"Morris does know art," said an otherwise quiet, gray-haired lady. "His workshops on conservation have been *wonderful.*"

Everyone looked at her as if she had just offended them.

"I wouldn't say he has too much appreciation for modern art," Tim Wyatt said. "He's more interested in preserving cultural memory than advancing with the times. He despises art as ideology. Never paid attention to politics."

"Why would he?" said Margie.

"A misanthrope," Wyatt sniffed. "When I had discussions with him about art, he would say that art is life—but what does that even mean? And what is life to him, living away from people like he does? He says the truth in life can only be preserved in art."

"But he's gay, right?" the balding man blurted out.

Margie burst out laughing, then stopped herself and looked for something to fan her face with. There was a stunned silence.

"Well," the balding man said, "he's never been married. Hey, have you seen my wife?" he added. He left the group, making his way with quick steps among the partiers.

In the group where he found his wife, Tommy Ryman was quiet for a while. Sarah Ryman, a mousy, graying woman, filled a glass for him. She pinched his cheek.

"Tommy! Where have you been, dear? We were just talking about you, and how long you've known Morris."

"Why do you all call him Morris?" asked a sober man dressed like the best man at a wedding.

"That's his last name, but it's better than Bill, a large, bearded man explained. "He'd have to be just a *tiny* bit more masculine to be a Bill."

"Morris is more artistic," explained his equally large wife, who had short, artificially red hair. She looked uncomfortable standing and, leaning on the table, she kept moving it and then pulling it back.

"Yes, Sarah Ryman said, 'Morris' is pretentious like someone working at a museum for forty years."

"Pretentious is not the word," Tommy Ryman said. "When someone's permanent mood is sarcasm, he better be named Morris."

"So what is the word then?" insisted his wife, holding him by the waist.

"He's here!" a nearby voice whispered. The words "He's here" traveled fast around the room. The choir of rumbling chatter imploded, leaving only small humming murmurs here and there.

Morris came through the door, smiling at everyone, and crossed the room while people made a corridor for him. He was dressed in a white suit, perfectly fitting his small, gracefully framed body.

"You've got a rabbit in the hat, Morris?" someone shouted. As Morris grinned, reassured laughter filled the room.

He reached a small podium he had placed at the center of the tables, which he'd arranged concentrically around it. The guests turned toward the podium. He surveyed the room. His eyes, softened by age under the perfectly white, thick hair, were still inscrutable, narrow and scornful. He was not exactly ugly, but his face was long, with disproportionately high cheekbones, while the drawn cheeks were too stretched even with the multiplicity of wrinkles. His lips, once thick, retained their crooked, protrusive exuberance of form that seemed designed by nature to offend. He grinned again, and his teeth, also, were too big. For a man of his small frame, his face appeared bigger than it should have been, which created an effect of drawing all attention to itself, perversely thwarting any attempts to ignore it—and him by extension.

"Let us, as Picasso put it, wash the dust of daily life from our souls," he started. "Thank you for being here—I know you are here for me and for me only, which is astounding, if I think about it. It is something I'm not sure I wished upon myself, but here we are, with the outline of years subtly stealing the life away from our faces."

A few murmurs, a few smiles encouraged him to go on. He paused for a moment, his gray, sharp eyes choosing a few people's faces upon which to linger uncomfortably. He picked an empty glass and poured himself a small amount of white wine.

"Thank God he's retired?" Morris teased. He lifted the glass. "Of course, I'm joking," he said, though his smile had something remote and painful in it. "I remember one year we held a special collections tour for a group of Chinese diplomats. There was one child with the group. Who would've thought? But it was that child who asked me a simple question: 'Do you paint, sir?' It was an extraordinary question because the child was visibly worried that he may not be speaking correctly and that his parents would disapprove, but he asked it anyway." He looked at the people nearest the podium. "Do you remember— does anyone remember what I answered? Tommy, do you remember?"

Tommy Ryman shook his head, and his wife whispered: "Think, Tommy! Does he paint?"

"You all know that our museum is a display of our cultural life operating at its best, yet no one who works there seems to be concerned about what we, the small people making it happen, what we may aspire to leave to the world, if we have sufficiently become a mix of public and private investment."

Puzzled faces, puzzled murmurs flared up for a few seconds.

"No, I don't expect you to remember what I answered to the little Chinese boy, whose concept of art, God knows, must have been an entirely different species than what we nurture here—our successive generations of increasingly abstract, increasingly bold artists, some gimmicky, some of them transcendent souls that I admire. In fact, this gathering today is also a tribute to them, the field dreamers, but also to that Chinese boy who seemed so suddenly concerned with whether I was appropriately fitted for that sacred place where art lives. To be fair, not everyone has talent. Are we to say that those who can't, organize exhibits? How about you, Miss Tanya," he asked of a young woman with sparkly eyes. "Do you paint?"

The woman blushed and shook her head. Morris was silent for a while.

"But let me not bore you anymore with speeches," he said. "I have only one more thing to say before—well, let's not anticipate. What I was leading up to with my story is a confession to you all, as we celebrate my retirement. I am not a braggart, which is why I've never told anyone about my passion. You may think, why would Morris, a quite boring fellow who works at a museum have secret aspirations as an artist, which he's never tried to use for his financial benefit or at least for that fleeting tremor of the inflated heart, which we call pride? It isn't really a surprise to any of you that I keep to myself, and I despise the crowding of the soul that comes with too much exposure. That is why, when I started developing an interest in painting, I didn't think I would ever show any of my work to anyone. But then I asked myself, if your paintings are life, should you not give back to life what you read *of* life, *within* life? The moments that I stole on my canvas, moments of ecstatic self-realization, should they not be returned to those who gave them to me? Which is precisely why I gathered you here, instead of going to Chuck E. Cheese's, as you might have planned for me."

"Come, Morris, say what you're trying to say," a few voices whinnied.

"Art is a gift. When life becomes so concentrated, so rewarding in one single moment that it crosses over into the sublime, something in you wants to give it back. That is why I want you to finally see the art I've created. Now, can I bother all of you to follow me? Take your glasses with you—you may need them."

With those words, Morris led the gathering through several rooms in his house, to a door that led to a large annex in his back yard—a whole other building, in fact. The first guests to enter gave out small cries of amazement and utter surprise: the annex was a small art museum, elegantly floored with quality wood, its rooms connected by large, doorless frames.

"Is this a replica of the museum, Morris?" Sarah Ryman said, breathless. "These are museum paintings! You copied them? They're perfect, Morris!"

"It is a replica, and it isn't. I've organized the three rooms based on the purpose of the paintings. Yes, the first room is my homage to a place I love, because it taught me that the people I work with are irrelevant, since art is what matters. How else would I have stuck it out working there?"

"Morris, we're not that bad, are we?" objected Margie.

"These are my favorite paintings at the museum. I have meticulously created reproductions of them, and I am quite proud of how close they are to their originals. Here is a Mary Cassat reproduction, although I've chosen to paint slightly more light around the human characters, to give more hope to the scene. Here," he pointed to an orange-filled scene of Civil War soldiers, "is my Trego."

After the awe at the first room was exhausted, he showed them the second room, on whose walls he had hung original work—mostly cityscapes with strange, larger than life birds hovering above buildings, humanized animals sitting on benches, large, fully clothed larvae crawling on sidewalks, and other anthropomorphic scenes in whose grim comic only he seemed to revel. Morris grunted and nodded as questions about meaning and symbols filled the room. He abstained from commentary, as wise artists tend to do when confronted with an outpour—genuine or any other variety—of curiosity.

"Please, let's all gather in the third room, which is where I hope to reach your souls, one way or another," Morris said, a sudden burst of light from a large window filling his face and leaving his distorted mouth, his haunted eyes in full display.

The guests looked at each other and their steps hesitated. By the time the last of them made it into the room, there already were gasps and angry shouts from the first people who had entered. Here, about twenty to thirty paintings adorned the well-lit walls. All the paintings, without fail, represented women—naked women—an absolute spectacle of mellow shapes and colors. Some were grotesque, yet there was beauty in every single one.

"Sarah, that's you!" Tommy Ryman was the first to exclaim what in the end became a refrain of male voices, each recognizing a wife, a lover, or merely a coworker.

Sarah Ryman's body was imperfect, with a slightly sagging stomach, yet her hair was not gray in the painting. Her shoulders were smooth and small, and her timid breasts, already in their declining years, were full of life as she tried to hide them with one hand. On her face, Morris had captured the fleeting joy of a moment, which few had ever seen, possibly not even her husband.

"Sarah, he's got the birthmark under your right breast right," said Tommy Ryman, his voice quivering like the voice of a child who dropped his ice cream to the ground.

"That's Mrs. Martin," someone whispered pointing at the wall. Just then, the small, bony woman ran out of the room, followed by her husband. "Would you have thought she had so many bones?"

"But it's still beautiful," someone murmured.

Right next to Mrs. Martin's painting was that of the large woman, whose bearded husband was now staring, unable to move or blink, at the flowing shapes of his wife in the frame. The generously padded buttocks rested on a large pillow, and the glowing-orange skin was spotted in places. It was beautiful. That was what the eyes of the remaining guests were saying, many blurred with their bewildered tears.

"I didn't pose—I wasn't posing," Margie said in front of a painting of the most exquisite, violin-shaped body, passion swelling every inch of flesh.

To the dwindling audience, Morris lifted his glass, scrutinizing the fallen faces, the free-flowing mélange of hurt made manifest either by guilt-like cowering or by useless anger.

"Thank you for my farewell party, my dear friends. Don't be ashamed of how you feel right now. Art begins and ends with being moved. After all, wasn't Paul Cezanne who said, a work of art that doesn't begin in emotion isn't art at all?" He looked around. His eyes maintained a steel composure.

The group scattered, retreated. The shouts of betrayed men exploded again outside the house, mimicking each other, yet each with its own palette of newly discovered disgust.

Morris was left in the middle of the last room. He was laughing—and not like someone who had just seen grown people fall on ice. It was as if something inside him had at last reached the world outside, and it really did find the world a funny thing.

Sound Waves

"And here you have it again, that canary voice I just can't let you forget. Vera Lynn, with her 1942 recording of 'The White Cliffs of Dover.' You're listening to our goldies hour, with your DJ, Charlie Tainter."

Nodding to the separating glass, he turned off the microphone and started the song, then pulled his earphones off. The violins' opening lines gilded the studio's walls with the intimacy of fresh snow and fireplaces. Vera Lynn's wavy voice took over, deepening the mood with the shadow-of-war, soft grayness of the first lines: *I'll never forget/ the people I met/ braving those angry skies—*

The DJ closed his eyes, leaning back in his chair.

In the control room, there was no piety.

"He's just *too* much into it," Danny said, holding his long chin. He reached for the sound board, slightly touching the blue tabs to push them higher, then pushed them down to about the same level as before. He grabbed his chin again.

"Stop messing with the pot. The mic is fine," said Rob. His gruff voice emerged from somewhere inside his big, gray mustache. His beer gut did not quite fit into the chair.

Danny straightened his back, carefully folding his bony hands in his lap.

"You don't think he's too obsessive about this 30's and 40's music deal?" Danny said. He adjusted his Bottega Velena cashmere hat and planted his blue suede Varvatos shoes up on the turret table, carefully avoiding the black, old-fashioned landline phone. He glanced at Rob, who pretended not to notice the boldness of the move.

"Say that to him and see if he gives you a full hour on air."

"I'm just saying. At least he should lay off the depressive stuff. Go for laughs, the 'Mad Dogs and Englishmen' with the cool accents, or those two guys with the Vader voice and the woman's voice, 'Jetsam and Flotsam?' Not the 80's thrash metal band, the older one." He sunk more into his legs-up position.

"You don't get it. Charlie was born to play this music. It's in his family. Been in his blood since the caveman."

"Yeah, DJ Caveman, right? Playing *I've Engraved 'I Love You' on This Tiger Tooth.*"

Rob shook his head. Over the tremulous voice of the singer, he signaled three fingers to DJ Tainter.

There'll be blue birds/ over the white cliffs of Dover/ tomorrow, just you wait and see.

"I guess it will still take me awhile to get used to all these signals," said Danny. He scratched his head lazily through the hat. "How long did it take you?"

"I don't remember, kid."

Rob's eyes moved up above the separating glass. He froze mid-nod. He smoothed his mustache with scratching sounds, then he pointed up.

"What?" said Danny. He turned to look at the frame on the wall—one of the grainy, old-stained photographs in the control room. This one was larger, different from the rest: it had a stern, bearded old man with a hat, while the others showed old family photos and country landscapes. "What are you pointing at?"

"I could've sworn the picture moved." Rob swallowed. His Adam's apple went up and down twice.

"The STL is too high, sends vibrations into the wall," Danny said.

"No." There was something less than reassuring in Rob's cheeks losing color. "There, it did it again."

"Just now? You mean it vibra— What the eff, man, what was that?"

"Damn right what the fuck," said Rob, standing up, and Danny followed.

The shepherd will tend his sheep/ the valley will bloom again, the song reminisced. The picture's vibration made a small, buzzing sound.

Both men took a step back.

Tomorrow, just you wait and see…

In the studio, the DJ looked at the separating glass. "This is your host, DJ Tainter, painting this enchanted hour with the tints of the past." A faint light illumined his face, and he tilted his head as if he'd seen something, or thought of something.

Rob sat down.

"Danny, sit down, we're freaking out Charlie."

The trumpets of a song filled the room, drowning the sound of the picture's vibrations. A homey duo began 'Underneath the Arches.' The picture was still again, but a few LED lights on the sound board flickered underneath it. The anomaly traveled down.

"Shit, they just fixed that," said Rob.

The flickering stopped somewhere close to the turret table. As their eyes reached the phone, it rang.

"Ah!" Danny jumped. "Crazy phone. *You* answer."

"What's the big deal?" Rob grumbled. He lifted the receiver. "This is WBGB, Boston's 90.1 Radio Station. Rob Trevor speaking." The phone was hissing. "Hello?"

Rob turned to Danny. His eyes looked lost.

"Somebody there?" Danny asked.

"Not really."

"Well, hang up."

He hung up. The phone rang again.

We dream our dreams away, bom-bom-bom-bop/underneath the arches, body-bom-bop, said the timeless duo.

"Yes? This is Rob Trevor."

There were a few beeps. Rob shook his head, and Danny reached and grabbed the receiver.

"Hello?" he said. The beeps became louder. Then, a voice.

"Mister Trevor?"

"No, this is Danny." He covered the receiver. "It's a *child*!" Again, into the phone, "Hello?"

There was a sigh.

"Hello? Are you there?"

"Um… You're talking?" the child said.

"Yes I'm talking! Who is this?"

"Hello?" The child sounded frightened.

Rob gestured to get the receiver back, glancing up at the picture. The picture was still and quiet now.

"This is 90.1, WBGB Radio," Rob said. "DJ Tainter's show. Why are you calling the station?"

"Charles Taa'inter?" said the boy. He couldn't have been older than ten.

"Yes Charlie Tainter. What do you want with the DJ? He's on air right now. Where are you, kid?"

No answer.

"Kid? I'm hanging up now." He did. He looked at Charlie behind the glass and saw him staring back. He turned in his chair, as the phone rang again. Danny picked up.

"Yes, hello?" he said.

"You have to say the radio station first," said Rob. "Should know that by now."

Standing, Danny glared at Rob and crossed his skinny legs in vintage Guess jeans, leaning on the metallic table.

"Kid, is that still you? Speak up."

"I am… I am Charles Taa'inter's son. Can I talk to my father?"

"What did he say?" Rob leaned in.

"It's Charlie's son," Danny whispered.

Rob looked sharply into the studio.

"What?" Danny whispered again.

"Charlie doesn't have any children," he whispered back.

…bom-body-bom… pavement is our pillow/no matter where we stray/ underneath the arches…

In the studio, Charlie was pacing.

"What's up with him?" Danny said to Rob, scratching his hat again. He looked at his shaky hands and stuck them in his back pockets. "Too much darn coffee," he muttered. Then, into the receiver, "What the heck, kid, who are you? Stop calling."

"And you stop hecking," Rob said, taking the phone from him.

"Hello? Charlie doesn't have any children."

"Hello?" The voice trembled. "Is my father there?"

The DJ was pressing his face against the glass now, palms spread on the sides like a mime's. His eyes were wide, his mouth shouting without sound. "Is my father there" had just been spoken loudly on the radio, over Jean Sablon's honey-mellow, plaintive *J'attendrai/le jour et la nuit/j'attendrai toujour/ton retour.*

"What did you do, *dumbass*?" Rob hissed, putting his headphones on and shouting a few reassurances into the small microphone.

"I didn't do that," Danny said.

Tainter's voice finally made it into the control room: "Don't you ever do that again." Yet his voice wasn't angry—just hurried and confused.

Rob and Danny looked at each other. They shook their heads.

The DJ finally sat back down. He was rocking to the sides, looking at the floor. Not in tune with the song. Danny realized he was still holding the receiver. He stared at it for a few seconds and put it to his ear.

"Kid?"

There was a long sigh on the other side. Then the child spoke again:

"He... Can you tell my father I'm in Mister Bell's lab—laboratory?" He sounded out every syllable, his voice wavy, watery.

"Look, he doesn't take calls at this hour," said Danny.

No answer. There was heavy breathing.

"Kid?"

"I am—" the child's voice broke, as if from crying.

"What *is* wrong with you, kid? Who in God's name *are* you?" He turned to Rob. "He sounds scared," he said. Then, to the phone, "Hey kid, what's your name? Can you hear me?"

"Aye. I'm Andrew Charles Taa'inter."

"No kidding. What's the problem? You can tell me, come on."

The boy was quiet.

"It's ok, nobody's mad at you, just tell me what's up."

"Excuse me?"

"This kid has a screw loose," Danny whispered to Rob. "What's *wrong*, Andrew? And what's with the funny accent?"

"I think... I think I've gotten into a bit of a bad show."

"A what? I don't know what you're saying, kid."

"It's my fault. Elsie took me to the laboratory and—"

Danny lifted his shoulders at Rob.

"—Elsie is Mister Bell's daughter," the child explained.

"Which Mister Bell?" said Danny. He leaned forward, with his elbows on the console.

"Mister Alec Bell. The photophone laboratory. With the telephony."

"What are you talking about, kid?"

"He makes *telephones*," the child said, desperate to be understood. "He was working on the photophone. I wanted to find a ship—"

"A ship?"

"—To see if I could hear a distress signal and save a sinking ship—I know the code, the Morse. Elsie said Mister Bell saved three ships already with the signal interception. But I spilled a cuppa… hot chocolate on the photophone and it beamed frightfully into the mirror on the magnetic wall, and Elsie said her father's going to proper kill me."

"Her father being—?"

"Mister Alexander Bell."

"As in, Alexander Graham Bell? So this is a prank, right kid? Enough of this now, we get it. Don't call back."

No answer. The child was crying. On the other side of the glass, an intense orange light had settled over Charlie's face, Charlie's desk. The microphone, the walls. Charlie's features were elongated with some kind of fear, and his mouth was half open. He stood up.

As the door opened and Charlie stormed into the control room, Danny quickly hung up. Charlie looked much taller on this side of the glass.

"Hi Charlie," Danny said. Rob crossed his arms and looked at the sound board.

"Morons!" Charlie blurted out. "Absolute morons. I'm having you fired."

"Oh come on, man. Did the kid sound on air again?" said Danny.

"Why aren't you in control over here? Playing with the fucking *lights* now? And—"

The phone rang. They all looked at it. Rob extended his arm to pick up, but Charlie was faster.

"DJ Tainter."

Danny looked at Rob. Rob coughed.

"Aye, can I speak with my father?" the child asked.

Charlie squinted hard at the phone. "Who are you looking for?" He looked at the picture on the wall, looked deep into it as if it would speak back. The big eyes in the picture were sunken in their sockets, just like his.

"Mister Charles Tainter, sir," said the eager voice on the phone.

Charlie covered his forehead, beads of sweat on his face.

"I'm playing some music here," he said, his voice a half-whisper. "Who put you up to this?"

The song had ended, and Charlie looked dumbly at the separating glass and blinked repeatedly. He lifted his arm as if to point to the glass with the receiver, then put it to his ear again.

"I have to play a song now," he said. "Don't call here again."

He stumbled to the door and rushed to the microphone, to turn it on. He sat down, wiping off his face with the back of his big hand.

"I'm going to play—" He laughed unconvincingly. "I'll play three songs in a row for you now, how about that? It's time for Bunny Berigan." He pushed the button and stood up.

He did not leave the room.

Left on the table, the phone let out a small, pleading voice. Danny shook his head and took a step back, so Rob finally picked up. The child was sobbing, still trying to explain.

"Mister Alexander Bell—he was tryin' to send the sound on a beam of light. Elsie heard it once at the magnetic—the mirror wall. It's the picture of my father. When I spilled the chocolate, the beam hit the picture and I think I did something to it. It was shaking. It keeps shaking. Can I speak with my father, sir?"

Rob's face darkened, as he bent over the table.

"My father—he's Mister Alec's assistant. He worked with him on the photophone—" The voice disappeared for a few seconds. "—more than the telephone, but he doesn't know if it will ever quite work."

Rob shook his head and said to Danny, without attempting to whisper, "Now he's talking about Alexander Bell again. *The* Alexander Bell?"

"—and a phonograph, and a flying machine, and I want to be an inventor like Mister Bell, but my father—"

"Say what now?" Rob tried again, sounding as if he'd given up.

"—Elsie—"

The voice hissed a few more seconds, then the sound stopped. The phone went silent.

"The kid's gone," Rob said matter-of-factly, yet with a hint of disappointment in his monotone.

Greta Garbo has had me to tea/ still I'm broken-hearted/ 'Cause I can't get started with you, sang Benny Berigan, but no one cared.

In the studio, DJ Tainter sat slumped in his chair, his back to the microphone.

"What was that about?" Danny said. "Charlie has a secret kid with schizo problems?"

"Maybe," Rob said.

"You said he has no kids."

"Hey, will you bring that frame down. I want to take a look at it."

Danny climbed on the metal table with the phone on it, and stretched his long arms above, grabbing the frame with both hands. With a few tugs, it came off the wall, leaving behind an empty discoloration. He lowered the frame, and Rob grabbed it carefully and set it on the floor.

"Flip it over, Danny."

"Charlie will be mad."

"Something's written on the back," Rob said, straining his eyes. "That's Charlie's writing. What's it say?"

"Says, *Charles Sumner Tainter. Cca 1885. My great-great-grandfather.* That's just messed up. So this guy in the picture is related to Charlie?"

"He got those pictures from a Genealogy Center. He says this one is his favorite, because this man was famous."

"Why is he famous, because he's the great-great-grandpa of a DJ?"

"I don't know, and I'm not gonna ask," said Rob, frowning to himself.

"Just a sec." Danny took out his iPhone. He buttoned for a while. "Seriously?" He pushed his hat all the way up to reveal his gelled, ruffled hair. He looked at Rob.

"What? You found something about his grandfather?"

"This is totally weird," Danny said and turned the iPhone to show Rob.

"I need reading glasses, buddy. Read it."

"So this is what's up. According to Wikipedia," he said and pulled his hat back on his forehead, "Charles Tainter *was an American scientific instrument maker, engineer and inventor, best known for his collaborations with Alexander Graham Bell.*"

The room was filled with the sounds of 30's blues, now lugubrious as if played directly from a cemetery. Rob opened his mouth but did not speak. Noiselessly, the door opened, the two still hunched over the picture. They looked up to face Charlie, now towering over them. He bent and snatched the frame, lifting it above their heads.

Rob stood and pulled up his ill-fitting khakis, then smoothed his mustache. Danny walked over to the console and busied himself.

"Charlie," Rob said, taking a fatherly tone. "You have to tell us, because this is messed up. Do you have a secret son?"

Danny looked up from the console. "Rob, don't."

"Shut up, Danny. Look Charlie, I don't want to interfere with family business and all, but I never knew you had any kids. And I'm sorry, but your kid is really strange. There's more—"

Charlie's face had lost all the blood.

"I have no kid!" he said, too fast. "Is it Betty who set this whole thing up? You're listening to Betty's bullshit? That kid is not mine—Was she on the phone too?"

The music sounded like deep silence. The notes of a trombone floated around the room pointlessly, with antique sadness.

"Say what?" said Rob.

Charlie looked at him as if they were both drunk.

"Stop this nonsense," Charlie whispered. "That kid of *hers* wants to be a DJ. That's no proof he is mine, you know? I have to go back. The song is ending."

He left the room. Watching him, they could have sworn he was staggering.

"The heck was that about? Who's Betty?" said Danny. "Look at this." He showed his iPhone to Rob.

Rob pushed the iPhone with his hand. "What?"

"Oh. Well it says here, *Tainter and Alec Bell worked together on a photophone, to transmit sound on a beam of light into a mirror, and they sent it two hundred feet away.* The kid, that's what the kid was saying."

"So?" Rob crossed his arms.

"I had this crazy idea that maybe the kid was right, that he was not *this* Charlie Tainter's son, *our* Charlie, but the *other* one's, the great-great—"

"Stop it. Don't you lose your mind too."

Danny looked at his iPhone, then at Rob. He gave a choked laugh.

"Yes, that would be too effed up."

"Danny, I'd say lay off the shrooms but I know you're a clean kid, so go back to the console. And not another word about it to Charlie. Subject's closed."

"Aye aye, Captain," said Danny. "Man, tell him to play Flat Foot Floogee, that hillbilly stuff. He's putting us to sleep big time."

"I thought you hipsters were more into garage bands."

Danny laughed. His face straightened with delayed hurt. Then he mock-punched Rob in the shoulder.

Rob grinned and nodded, his walrus mustache bobbing to the gentle rhythm of the song.

Danny had not read the entirety of the Wikipedia entry about Charlie Tainter. *In 1885,* said the part he hadn't finished reading, *his young son was caught playing in Alexander Graham Bell's photophone laboratory and notoriously took a beating from his father, which he would later write about in his memoirs.*

According to a footnote, a child named Andrew dreamed of saving drowning people from frozen seas. He took a beating for it. Years later, he would fall in love with the radio.

Warner's Caddy

I fill the buckets with water and I take them to the stalls, one stall at a time. My boots thump on the hardened dirt floor.

How did I let Dan talk me into this?

Just that morning, he told me I would be helping him write the names of those who bought raffle tickets for the Cadillac, to save the horse business from bankruptcy. *That* Cadillac, the "new, only driven a few times in ten years" Cadillac that has been sitting in the grass by the barn door the whole time I've worked at the stable. He even tried to teach me to drive it once, and I almost backed it into the barn.

With the raffle tickets, he ran such a campaign with me that, against my better instincts, I did, in fact, talk to students in my classes, to get them to pay twenty dollars for a ticket. I sold two. Two other friends sent twenty dollars from Maryland, one of whom was my Faulkner professor who was born on a ranch in Montana. He sounded pretty sure he wouldn't really win a Cadillac. I bought three tickets myself. I still have a huge stack of tickets, and the pig roast and raffle are tomorrow.

The line he sold me on was the heartbreaking "if I go bankrupt the state will sell the horses to dog food companies." I did ask him why he didn't just sell half of the horses, or all of them, and retire, and he said there was no other way he would live the rest of his life than on that farm, doing what he was doing. He said if he did go bankrupt he'd be waiting here, in his house, with a gun, and he would go down in flames. I know he's not lying because he does have a gun for every square foot of the house. I counted thirty downstairs, and I'm sure he has more upstairs where he sleeps. Two rifles (I hope they're not loaded and I have no clue how to check) are what I use at night to secure the dirty curtain that passes for a door in the room where I sleep. Not that I'm afraid—he would have raped me a month ago when I came into his house, if he'd really wanted to. I just don't want him to be able to see in my room, though he says he's seen it all in his time. At this point (two days before I leave), there's nothing left of the fear I came here with, the one that gave me a big-time nightmare on the first night.

No, I'm not afraid of him. I don't quite know what he is to me. He's a 59-year-old close to bankruptcy, with twenty horses whose names and habits I can recite in my sleep and whose manure (he calls it horseshit, of course) I've been shoveling for a month because I really wanted to work on a farm and "learn about horses." How many times must he have scorned city people for giving him that line. I've been living in his house because I don't have a car to drive back and forth every day. He brought me here in his old truck just before it stopped working.

The raffle tickets. As I promised, I tear the paper out of the notebook he handed me, and I tear each page into smaller sheets. I start writing the names carefully, one for Patrick from Kenya, one for the Chinese student, the quiet-weird-international-student-from-communist-country just like me, who I knew would not have said no to me. Three tickets for me. One for the Maryland professor who loves horses and Faulkner. One more for the other friend. About fifty more for whoever bought them from Dan.

Dan has put on his glasses and now he lost a little of the look that spells angry cowboy who will shoot you five times without even looking, a cigarette in the corner of his mouth. He watches me calmly over the dusty boxes and tools and stacks of dishes on the kitchen table (if you're going to use them, you're going to need them where you eat, he says). It's the only table in the house with room to put something on it. I finish writing the names he gave me, and now he says what I dreaded he would say.

"Now make up some names."

I can't believe I let Dan talk me into this. I did suspect he wasn't really going to let the Cadillac (worth at least three thousand, he says) go to one of the fifty-sixty people who paid twenty dollars. And, let's face it, some of it is my fault for not convincing thousands of students and professors at the university to buy raffle tickets for a Cadillac on a horse farm, so I did expect him to do something about such slim pickings. I just wasn't sure in what way he would involve me. Would he shoot the person who won the Cadillac and ask me to help dig a grave? Not too plausible, since he proved sane enough not to rape his twenty-something-year-old female help, whom he repeatedly asked to smoke pot with him so she'd "jump into my lap like all women who smoke pot." He would not be any less sane about shooting people for a car. He would shoot the authorities if they came to get his horses, that's what he says, but he would not kill for a car.

"But, Dan, I can't do it. You want me to lie to the people who are coming to the pig roast?"

"They'll still have a chance," he mumbles, coughing. "We just need about two hundred other names, so we have more to draw from."

My nice-girl upbringing is squirming and cringing inside, and just then he gives the final blow to what's left of my idealism.

"If you don't do it, I'll have to do it myself. And my hands ache. See, they shake. Your handwriting is better than mine."

If I don't do it, it will get done anyway, I tell myself. I am not the engine to the crumbling of great principles. He's the one doing it. I'm just helping him, not the action itself. Just as I did with the marijuana plants.

At the beginning, the same cringing, squirming voice raised objections: I can't carry water through the woods to the marijuana plants. It would be as if

I were growing them myself. I'm watering them, so I'm an accessory to crime. Drug cartels, the voice said. Decapitated people. Child labor. Smuggling. Marijuana plants. Now *I am growing* marijuana.

That voice went away when I explained to it, look, Dan would carry twenty gallons of water in each hand by himself, four times instead of two, and even if he is stronger than you because he piles the horseshit higher than you in the wheelbarrow, he is frail, he has worked hard for many years, and took care of twenty horses by himself after his second wife, Jerry, left him because "she could not take it anymore" (Dan still doesn't know what she meant, and I try not to imagine too much past his rough stubbornness). He shoveled horseshit and carried bales of hay from truck to barn to field, from truck to barn to field, brushing horses, saddling them, as grumpy with them as he is with people, for sixteen years. That's what he told me. Sixteen years ago, that was when he could no longer be an engineer—it made him a pretty penny, but he couldn't stand working for other people anymore, not without constantly getting into fights and seeing the inside of jails a little too often, and screwing up his liver with alcohol because he did not feel free.

Then he started working for a big horseback riding business, where he kept his horse, at Pleasant Hill. He hated the way they treated the horses there—put too many in a stall, put heavy people on small horses and some of the employees rode bareback, bending the horses' backs. Using English saddles instead of Western, the tiny English saddles on which they trot like pompous fools pounding on the back of the horse instead of riding *with* the horse, as cowboys do, as he learned long ago from Arizona cowboys who ride on Western saddles to distribute their weight evenly over the backs of the animals. This makes him the only true cowboy in Upstate New York.

That was also when his first wife divorced him.

He decided then to use all his savings to build his horse business, and he swore he would charge less than the big stables, and treat the horses better, and he bought the land and cleared with his own hands the path through the woods, so people would enjoy their ride and get a bit of everything: go down the path while learning to lean back to help the horse keep its balance, then go through a tricky clearing that isn't actually his land but it's ok because it's just a small clearing, then go up the hill and across a field with many crows flying around, where the horses feel like running, but "you never let them run the horses!" as he said, one of the many things he yelled at me as he taught me how to be a trail guide. Then back through the woods and back to the barn.

I helped him carry the buckets of water through the woods and we had to bend before getting to the trees, because bushes were too low and drivers on the road would see us and figure out what we were doing because people just know what buckets with water are needed for, when you go into the woods.

Most farmers grow marijuana, he said, but for him, he said, it's a necessity. It's just that little bit of extra income that keeps the horses from going to the dog food factory. He's planning something bigger than this, like renting one of the fields for an amusement park, but until then he'll just grow and sell marijuana.

That's how, in my mind, the watering of the plants has become a sacred ritual, something as pure as the sight of horses on the field early in the morning, eating hay and running through the mist that lifts and joins the big swirls gathering above the treetops. Pure like the mist between those two hills that he showed me the first day, at five thirty in the morning when we took the wheelbarrows to the path in the woods, to dump the crap and fill the holes made by rain, so the horses wouldn't trip.

The secret place with the marijuana plants was hard to reach, because he left the thorny, spidery bushes around them on purpose, so no one would find them. The palmed plants smelled and looked like Christmas trees, and I felt as if we were going to pick one for the house. We are such a team, he said, we are like a married couple except for the sex. I always laugh to myself hearing that, because I still have no idea how I managed to dodge his advances, living in his house as I do, with the first neighbors half a mile away down the hill. Haifa, my Syrian roommate, nearly fainted when he came to pick me up at the apartment, his grumpy, skinny self, eyes of steel, and jeans that seemed to have survived his very return from Vietnam.

The marijuana plants were gone before the Cadillac raffle and the pig roast. A few days ago, he left me driving the tractor in the field where he gave riding lessons, and went to check on the plants. When he came back, I could not even tell him proudly that I had hit a rock while cutting the grass and the big screw was busted, so I replaced it just as he'd shown me. Me, mechanically challenged, without a driver's license. I could not tell him, because his face was grimmer than the day when he thought Dusty, his Arabian horse, was dying, and we had to walk the horse for six hours to get his cramps to cease.

"The neighbor stole the marijuana plants," he said, and his eyes of blue steel, the same eyes that scared his neighbors' children under the table when he stopped by, were not even looking at me.

"How do you know it was your neighbor?"

"He's been eyeing the plants, I've seen him. He stole them while we were out on the two-hour ride. Stole two out of the three patches. Cut all the plants clean off the ground."

"So go get it back."

"He won't admit he did it. I can't call the police on him, can I," he said, and something earthy, something defeated but not done was in his voice. He did not even sound like a man whose only source of extra income was gone, and he was closer to bankruptcy than ever. He sounded just like that, like life. Things come, things go.

That's when he put a gun in my hand, and I wasn't sure if it had come from downstairs, from my room, maybe, or from upstairs, where perhaps he kept the loaded ones. I told him I didn't want to take the gun. To do what with it?

"Go saddle Tyler. We're going to start on the two-hour path, so he'll think we're going for two hours. Then we cut through the woods on a path I know, and we catch him in the act. He'll try to get the third patch for sure."

"And if he sees us with guns, who do you think he's going to shoot first? I'll be like a clown carrying a gun, saying please shoot me."

"Nah, he won't try. If he does, I'll take him down."

That's Dan.

I talked him out of giving me the gun (he decided I shouldn't hold it because I didn't have a permit), but I didn't talk him out of riding our horses to sneak up on his neighbor, the thief. I knew it wouldn't turn out as well as a Clint Eastwood movie, or at least not for me, were we to find the man cutting the marijuana plants. If this neighbor had the crazy eye like Dan, I'd be toast anyway, carrying a gun or not. Yes, I had met some of his neighbors, including one cop who smoked pot with Dan and the others, and when they tried to pass it to me, I said no, and Dan had to reassure them, she's cool. I had never had pot before, and of course I could not forget that "women jump into my lap when they smoke pot with me," so I never smoked it.

The neighbor was not there. Instead, Dan cut the plants down himself, and we carried them to the house. All ten of them. That night, my hands were sticky and green from separating buds from leaves and stems with scissors. My hands smelled wonderful.

That's how Dan talks me into things.

So I'm writing the names. We compromised to a hundred and fifty of them. Thankfully, I don't have to think of too many variations, as he says he'll only draw once, so I can write one single name a hundred times or more. I choose the name of this cool poet from Maryland, the professor who writes about life in charming ways, mixing the metaphors with wonderful images of trees and goldenrod flowers. I picked goldenrod with Dan, when I convinced him that the flowers were good for stomach aches, taken as a tea. That's when he said, see, you learn a lot of new things from me, and I learn a lot from you. You have knowledge from your books, and I have practical knowledge.

Goldenrod makes the fields smell like bees and sun when the morning loses its chill.

I write: Michael Warner, Michael Warner, Michael Warner... He watches me from behind those glasses that look misplaced on the face of a cowboy. Even in the house, he never parts with his gray hat, and he wants me to keep mine on. He gave it to me on my first day here, because I'd be in the sun all day. It belonged to Jerry, who left him three years ago, and she was about the same size as me. My hat is gray too, except mine is limp and deformed and it didn't get in shape even when we tried to steam it at the stove, boiling a pot of water. His hat is sturdy, good quality. For all I know, the hat survived Vietnam too—maybe that secret mission where he killed people at close range, with a knife. It's sticky, he says, blood gets all over you. So he says, and I've learned that I'll never be able to tell between his true stories and his bullshit stories.

I wake up before him, on the day of the pig roast. At night, I sleep in my pajamas, but when I hear him coughing I know it's about time, and I put my day clothes on. He asks me if I sleep in my day clothes. I don't mind that I haven't washed any of my clothes the whole time I've been there because, to be frank, he didn't even put clean sheets on the bed in honor of my arrival, so when I sleep I curl away from the crumpled sheets, trying not to smell the old mattress and covering myself with an old, stained blanket. Hell, I only took a shower twice this whole month, and now I smell like everything else: horses, and a hundred-year-old house. How can I take showers when the door to the bathroom is also a dirty curtain that doesn't stay in place. And he's always around, everywhere I go. When Haifa, my roommate, sees me again (and smells me), she may actually faint.

Haifa is not coming to the pig roast, but Dong-Xin, the shy Chinese girl is. So is Patrick, the guy from Kenya who bought the other raffle ticket. It's only half a pig, Dan said, because there won't be enough people there to be worth paying for a whole one. But he'll teach me to cut the meat right out of the red embers, with the buck knife he gave me (he said to keep it, even if it didn't belong to Jerry).

We even had some trail rides in the morning and early afternoon, so as he's getting the roasting oven ready next to the wire fence where we throw the hay for the horses, I take the small riding parties out for the one-hour ride. I haven't graduated to the two-hour ride. I can't go on it without him, because as he said the first time I asked him what I should be aware of, as a trail guide, he said, anything can happen. *Anything.* That's something I keep in mind every time I go on the one-hour trail, turning, as he told me, to look at every person behind me and make sure they're not falling off or letting the horses eat, trying to get impatient little Tyler to wait for them. Good old Tyler, who got used to me even if he's the horse who bucked me off the most since I've been here. He used to spin so I couldn't get on, with people there waiting for me to take them on the trail, losing business for Dan when a little girl didn't want to go anymore because she saw me fall. Falling is overrated.

Now I love the little horse and I hug him because he's small enough that I can press my face into his yellow hair, and I smell hay and spunk, mixed in with that smell that is common to all horses. Dan laughs at me for hugging a shithead (all his horses are shitheads), and he laughs when I tell him I talk to Tyler in Romanian.

"What an idea," he says, as he laughs. "They only know English."

By the time my last ride is back, there are many people at the ranch already. Some are playing horseshoe-tossing, and Dan wants me to go try it too.

"You'll like it for sure," Dan says. "It's your kind of game."

I don't know what that means, but I give it a try, and I get beaten by jovial, round-faced people. And their children.

I show Dong-Xin around, though I don't want to scare her by taking her into the house. It's enough that she sees the raggedy barn, though she says it's exciting. Patrick makes jokes, and some are about me being there alone with Dan all this time. I shrug them off. I've gotten used to people assuming I'm sleeping with Dan, and I don't even care anymore. It only hurt when Doug thought that, and I saw it on his face before he stopped coming to ride here. Doug worked for Dan before me, and he even had a horse at his stable, until he moved out of town when he got back together with his girlfriend. He looked like a strangely misplaced, blond musketeer, with the manners of a musketeer. He will probably marry her, from what he mumbled to Dan and me when he came to take his horse.

The day goes by fast. When night falls, people are animated and surround the bonfire. Stories flow, to the sound of crackling wood and night birds. The hills are one with the dark sky, but I can guess where they are and where the fog will be tomorrow.

I impale the meat on my buck knife and join Dong-Xin and Patrick by the fire. This is the solemn time when Dan draws from a hat. I've shown Dong-Xin the Cadillac even if she doesn't have a driver's license either. If she wins, she can sell it and pay six months' worth of rent. If I win, I won't have to worry about saving money to fly home. I have three chances. She has one.

When Dan brings the stack of papers I folded the day before, I try not to cringe. Again. There are fewer than I remember stacking, and I have good visual memory. I almost feel as if I remember how I folded each paper, and I imagine the names written inside. I know now: he was never going to include the real names, the ones of the people I had talked into buying raffle tickets. My horse-loving professor and my other Maryland friend, and these two who are smiling broadly right next to me, waiting to win an American car.

I bend my head. I know what's coming. The thirty-odd people look at him with benevolent eyes, and I can see that they know too. They smile. They don't want him to lose the farm.

He draws from his gray hat.

"Michael Warner," he announces.

People look around, as if expecting a Michael Warner to come and claim the Cadillac.

Dan waits, while I stare at the fire.

"He didn't show up, what do you know," says Dan. "I'll have to call him tomorrow."

Bankruptcy takes one small step back. The pig roast goes on.

ACKNOWLEDGMENTS

I would not have written at least half of these stories without LitReactor, where I learned to be competitive, to surprise myself with the directions my writing took, to hone my craft through the generosity of my fellow writers and our instructors. I am grateful to Mark Vanderpool, Craig Clevenger, Christopher Bram, Lidia Yuknavitch, writers from whom I learned directly, and also to authors who inspired me, such as Gabriel Garcia Marquez, Cormac McCarthy, Toni Morrison, Chuck Palahniuk, Leslie Marmon Silko, William Faulkner, and so many others.

I am also thankful to my husband, Robin Andreasen, who is always my first reader, and to my sister, my brother, my mother, and my friends near and far, whose encouragement always helped me dream big and not give up on myself.

Liana Vrăjitoru Andreasen started publishing short stories in her early 20s, as a student in Romania. For a time, her creative writing took a back seat during her graduate studies in Maryland and New York State, when she felt she had to crack the code of the playful, cryptic theories that were fashionable at the time, such as deconstruction and poststructuralism. Teaching college English in Texas brought her back to the real world, where she searched for ways to connect her love of literature and criticism, her work with students in a vibrant, diverse community, and her philosophical inclinations. Not willing to give up on her creativity, she became part of LitReactor, a writers group formed under the wing of Chuck Palahniuk. Her fiction began to thrive in this rich creative soil, where she finally found her voice as she started to take more risks.

Endlessly fascinated by the way in which her native and her adoptive cultures clash and merge within her identity, she sees herself as a nomadic soul with stories to tell, and she absorbs reality into her own prisms, creating a fictional world of multiplicities.

The stories tap into the mysteries of the unconscious and of the inscrutable threads that connect us. Whether through magical realism ("Whirl of Birds," "Stolen Light," "Valley of the Horse"), through symbol-rich, poignant realism ("Away from the Flock," "At Taft Point," "Driving with Sara"), creative nonfiction ("Warner's Caddy"), or even science fiction ("Sound Waves" and "Prodigal"), what all stories have in common is that their characters fight hard for the kernel of hope that sometimes appears out of reach. Navigating through an assortment of pitfalls—deep poverty, magnified egos, time travel, suicide cults, mental illness—not all characters come out unscathed. The recognition of another's humanity is embedded in the characters' pursuit of self-actualization, whether a failure or a success.

All the stories in this collection have first found a home in literary journals over the last decade or so, and some have been slightly edited after their first publication. Journals such as *The Quail Bell, Fiction International, Scintilla,* Mensa's *Calliope, Lumina, Eureka Literary Magazine, Adelaide Literary Magazine, Mobius, a Journal of Social Change, Blue Hour,* and many others, have at various times published Liana Vrăjitoru Andreasen's short stories. In 2017, she published with BlackWaterpress *The Fall of Literary Theory,* a book of literary criticism, and she has also published many critical essays, book reviews, and translations of poetry and fiction. She was a principal editor for the literary journals *Interstice* and *Sleipnir,* and she has been a long-time collaborator with the Romanian journal *Alecart.*